RISE AND SHINE

10 keys to spectacular success

MANLION AUTHOR SOLUTIONS

First Published in October 2020

Published by:
Manlion Author Solutions

Powered by:
Kalon Maple Publishing

Distribution by: Pothi.com

ISBN: 978-81-947268-4-5
Price: ₹199

Layout and cover design:
Mrunaal Gawhande (Kalon Maple Publishing)

Distributed by:
Paperback: amazon.com, amazon.in, flipkart, Pothi.com
E-Book: amazon.in/com, apple (ibooks stores in 51 countries), Barnes & Noble (US and UK), Scribd, Kobo, and Blio, Overdrive (World's largest library ebook platform serving 20,000 + libraries), Baker & Taylor Axis 360, Tolino, Gardners, Google Play Books, Bibliotheca Cloud Library (3,000 public libraries) and Odilo.

CONTENTS

Foreword

By Brigadier Sushil Bhasin

Brigadier Sushil Bhasin

is a time investment strategist, global speaker, and author of
three books including 'Million Dollar Second' published by CNBC.
He is a proud protégé of Speakers Institute. A TEDx speaker, and
corporate trainer, he has a mission to create a world conscious of
time as a vital resource. He delivers 'High Impact Virtual
Engagement' webinars.
www.BrigSushilBhasin.com
sushil@BrigSushilBhasin.com

Making every second count

The foreword, I presume, will be read before the rest of book. Just like the 10 authors who have some profoundly insightful things to say about self-refinement, I am doing my bit to set the pace for the pages that will follow this one. I am writing on a topic that impacts all the others mentioned in this book – time! The lines that follow are on creating a time-abundant life, where you are never too busy.

It is a life where you have loads of time to do whatever you please. We need to revisit the subject of managing, investing and creating time because we are living in the middle of the most-widespread epidemic humankind has ever known.

This new normal has turned our homes into offices. It has made the virtual more real. Everything from the dress code, bathing, shaving rituals, child-rearing, and education has changed for most of us. Work as well as education are being home delivered to our drawing rooms and bedrooms. It is imperative that we revisit how time is accounted for, utilized, and invested by individuals, families, businesses, and societies. Businesses that involve the assembly of humans at one place like schools, playgrounds, public transport terminals, and activities that call for intimate human touch like the preparation of food and its distribution have changed forever. As a time abundance trainer, improving efficiencies and inculcating behaviors that magically create more time available to people is my primary concern. Given the situation we are in due to the protracted lockdowns, work-from-home and the partial halting of the public transport system, we should have had more time.

The truth is that even those who are no longer travelling are experiencing that they have even less time than they had earlier.

This is happening because we have not only permitted the office to invade our house, we have also allowed it to eat into hours beyond what used to be our routine workday.

Whether this is done because bosses are demanding it, or because we are ourselves working at a pace that has allowed this to happen, the result is that many among us are shorter of time than we have ever been.

At the heart of the time-creating strategies that I teach is the creation of efficiencies in individual, familial, social and corporate processes. These efficiencies are caused by a formula I call the signing of the PDC (Problem Solving + Delegation + Compassion).

Problem solving + Delegation + Compassion = Efficiency

> An example of problem-solving would be to reduce attrition by arranging home pickups and drops for employees living in cities with overburdened transport systems.

> Delegation is the act of offloading part of one's work that offers low ROTI (Return on time invested) to someone else so one can create more time for stuff that offers higher ROTI. Wasting valuable time in micromanaging stuff that can be delegated is not an intelligent thing to do.

> Compassion has to do with viewing colleagues as human beings and not just as human resources. Human beings have needs like the education of children, housing, and health that corporate entities can solve at cheaper rates and save time, money, and effort for colleagues who are contributing to the growth story of the brand.

A willingness to solve problems, to delegate and the exercise of compassion combine to create a culture of efficiency, which I call a time-abundant culture because it saves a lot of time. It is self-evident that all members of a team who are part of such a time abundant culture are in a position to get more done in more time.

Creating such a time abundant culture takes a series of actions that are beyond the scope of this small piece but here are a few steps you can take right now to usher time abundance in a small measure in your life right now.

So, here are my five 'to-dos' that will long way towards creating time abundance in your life in the post-COVID world.

1. Limit screen time/ Work less: Most of us who were used to checking our phones first thing in the morning on waking and the last thing before calling it a day have overwhelmed ourselves with too much time before the screen. Six hours with a screen guard and hourly breaks is the most anyone should be doing.

2. Become online-savvy: Raise your awareness of online tools that can help you save time. The COVID virus has forced people to explore options online and made people realize that a lot of locomotion is avoidable to get the job done. Even after the virus has been defeated, the virtual world will continue to become more real in all aspects of life. Ensure that you familiarise and use all available tools to 'create' more time.

3. Love your mate: And your parents, and kids. If you are working from home, ensure that you are not so overwhelmed by work that it impacts family time. With kids home, you are probably among those shouldering the responsibility of ensuring that the time table is followed diligently by the kids on google classrooms. Be conscious in your loving. Be love.

4. Make it a season of learning and giving: I have contributed as an author to five different books during the lockdown, three of which are with groups of authors who have decided to donate all revenues from sales of the books worldwide to charity. It is a very good time to reach out, support and make a difference. Give karma a reason to smile upon you, Find a way of making a difference.

5. Exercise: Lack of physical movement has unwelcome consequences for your mental and physical health and on our relationship with your family and your workplace. Find ways of becoming efficient that makes it possible for you 'create more time'. Do not forget that sitting the new smoking. Its cumulative effect can be fatal.

Be solutions-driven, delegate whatever you can, and take compassionate action to make life easier for your own self, colleagues, company and your customers.

Happy PDC, friends!

Introduction

By Jogesh Jain

Jogesh Jain
is the founder of JJ School of Employability and
MakingIndiaEmployable.com

At the heart of rising and shining

It is only in our darkest hours that we may discover the true strength of the brilliant light within ourselves that can never, ever, be dimmed.

Doe Zantamata

This is a tough time. It is a time that challenges us to 'Rise and Shine'. Had it not been for this time, there are so many lessons that have come to us that we would have missed. I shall share some of the 'Rise and Shine' lessons that I have learned in this time when it comes to my core area of focus – employability.

It is human nature to constantly seek growth.

If we do not have the desire to seek growth, we have clearly lost touch with our true organic selves because it is the nature of 'being' to constantly expand. And the way it works is that if you are not expanding you are contracting. A gym is a good metaphor for the world as a place to develop our talent muscles. When we eat right, rest right, and exercise right, the muscles grow. The moment I slip into my old ways of senseless eating and sedentary habits, I start losing the muscle mass that we have built with a lot of effort and sacrifice.

What do the words Rise and Shine mean to me as an employability coach?

Just as employability goes way beyond the ability to land a job, and is about the degree to which one can provide value to a professional ecosystem, rising and shining is more about awakening to one's true nature and radiating that nature out in the world than it is about waking up in the morning and brightening the world with our presence.

Once this happens, the life meant for you easily manifests.

I recognize the current downturn caused by COVID 19 as an opportunity because I recognize that all breakdowns herald a season of breakthroughs and I have numerous stories from my own life to prove it.

I had failed the seventh grade when I was not yet in my teens.

It was a shock, which, in hindsight, had a welcome fallout. It made me revisit the way I had been studying, the impact it was making in my life and the prospects it held for my future. I had been a vernacualar-medium school student. where the atmosphere was not conducive for me. After much deliberation, it was decided that I would not only change schools but that school would be an English Medium School. This added to my difficulties but I was given additional coaching to address my learning challenges, and slowly but surely, I did turn my life around.

I look back with gratitude for the things that I learned in the years that followed. Had the shock of failure not come my way, I would have continued with my school the way it had been.

This was an early lesson in the value of obstacles or setbacks in helping me rise and shine.

Moving to Mumbai was another such shock for me. I was comfortable in my hometown, which is where all my friends were at that point. It was also a place where all treasured memories of my life had been created. I have spent a decade-and-a-half in Mumbai, which has given me so much. I have struck gold in many ways that would not have been possible if I had stayed back. However before success arrived with the success of JJ School of Employability, there was a phase when I was not even able to pay my domestic bills.

There came a day, when, after returning from a wedding function, I had to explain to my son who was not yet three why every other apartment other than ours had electricity. My response was to smile in the darkness.

Would you like to know why?

While this was a testing time and money was scarce, with the opening of the JJ School of Employability, I was finally aligned with my true purpose, which in turn, was aligned with my true nature. Standing in that darkness, I knew that it was just a matter of time before I would rise and shine.

This lockdown is just another of those times.

Friends, wherever you are in your life, this is what I wish to tell you - never forget that every challenge thrown at you is but an opportunity to bounce forward. That fellow traveler is the core, the central, the heart-of-the-heart insight of this book - Rise and Shine!

Aarti Bharj

is a certified NLP practitioner, life coach and clinical psychologist. She is a trained counsellor with years of experience in leading the transformation of people struggling with life issues, relationships, anxiety, and depression. She is certified in Arhatic Yoga and Pranic Psychotherapy by the World Pranic Healing Foundation, Manila. She is also a Yoga and meditation instructor, a transformation coach and a relationship consultant. She combines the principles of humanistic counselling, coaching, and energy therapy, in her sessions. She is a founder member of 'Spruaa Life Coaching' and an anchor on the YouTube channel by the same name. Through her program 'New Horizons, New Challenges' she guides young adults struggling with career choices, addictions and relationship issues.

She has experience of over 19 years in the software industry. She has worked as a Software Architect with many renowned MNCs before she decided to dedicate herself to helping society. She is associated with many NGOs and is the secretary of 'We Together Foundation – Grain Bank Concept'. She is also a trained kathak dancer and conducts dance workshops for underprivileged children and dance therapy sessions for kids with intellectual disabilities.

She is a sought-after speaker at various cultural events.

1. Are You Crisis Cool?

By Aarti Bharj

All Birds find shelter during the rain. But the eagle avoids rain by flying above the clouds.

APJ Abdul Kalam

A crisis is a critical moment in a person's life, a crucial or decisive situation that requires a solution swiftly to sail through it. The noun 'crisis' comes from the Latinized form of the Greek word 'krisis', meaning "turning point". It is a make or break moment, based on a person's response to the situation.

A psychological crisis is a life event that an individual perceives as stressful to the extent that normal coping mechanisms are insufficient. It may turn into a catastrophe for a person if not handled on time. As an example, Coronavirus (Covid-19) pandemic has swept the world, causing widespread concern, fear and stress. But whether this turns out to be a period of crisis for you or not, depends on the way you choose to respond to this challenging situation.

The world is expected to be in a heightened state of emotional flux in the years to come. The World Health Assembly, Geneva, in a policy briefing has urged the international community to do much more to protect all those facing mounting mental pressures and emotional health issues. A crisis can arise due to various factors such as increased stress, financial strain, relationship conflict, health issues or disease, exposure to traumatic incidences. Let us look at a few cases.

Scene 1: It is SCC result day. Aditi feels more and more anxious as the scheduled time for online results declaration approaches. Aditi is a bright student with a good track record. The whole family gathers around her father's laptop, excited.

They log into the site. The hourglass keeps rotating for some time, deepening Aditi's distress. As she stares at the screen, her face turns white and her palms started sweating. Her mother screams, "No! this can't be her! Log in again." Her father does what he has been ordered.

It is the same score!

The whole house goes into a mourning mode. Relatives keep calling in. Mobiles of all family members keep buzzing, unanswered. They do not wish to convey to anyone that Aditi, a class topper, had just scored 89%. Her dreams of becoming a world-class software engineer appear to be shattered, Aditi eats no food that entire day. She locks herself in her room with the lights switched off. She stares into the darkness. She keeps blaming herself for bringing shame to her family.

At 8 p.m. Akshay, her elder brother, knocks on the door. She does not open it. He keeps knocking, calling out her name in a soft, kind voice. She opens the door after a few minutes. Akshay is standing there with a packet of chocolates and a smile. She refuses to have any. Akshay opens the pack and feeds a piece to his little sister.

"Congratulations," he says.
Aditi starts crying loudly in his arms. He let her vent without saying a word.

Is this a real crisis or a perceived one?
Do you think Aditi would have suffered more or taken an extreme step, had Akshay not intervened?

Emotional Health: Emotional health is a person's ability to accept and manage his or her feelings through challenge and change. When the subjective experience of emotions is appropriate over a sustained period, emotional health is thought to be present. Emotional health includes both emotional intelligence and emotional regulation.

The mundane hassles of daily life offer opportunities to practice responses rather than reactions and allow emotional health to flourish. During a crisis, emotional health can get seriously affected.

Someone suppressing emotions, especially from childhood, may not be as emotionally healthy as someone vulnerable enough to express their emotions. The experience of an emotion is reflected by changes in speech, body, and face. For example, a person who experiences joy may speak loudly, make a lot of gestures, and face of a person experiencing negativity may be pale, with shoulders drooping. External factors affect emotional health.

Scene 2: Sheila was walking towards the parking lot after a long 16-hour duty as Head Nurse at the City Hospital. Covid-19 infections kept increasing every day exerting immense pressure on the healthcare facilities. It was difficult to even sip water with the PPE gear on. It was tiring, exhausting and joyless work. Sometimes the nurses would be so exhausted they would sleep in the hospital itself rather than going home and taking the complicated and time-consuming clean up the ritual to be undertaken before touching their loved ones. Some days and nights they would not even have a chance to catch up few hours of sleep at a stretch and some had not seen their own families for months together. Sheila was living in the government quarters nearby and hence was lucky enough to go home every day at least for a few hours and meet her young kids.

As she was walking, she noticed ward boys and clean up a taskforce with the huge burden of eliminating bodies of patients who died due to Covid-19. They had to be wrapped properly and labelled and handed over to the relatives. Many times, the relatives would not turn up to collect the body and there would be no place left in hospital morgue to keep them. As a result, heaps of dead bodies would be lying on the road unattended, wrapped, and waiting for a funeral. The sight, the smell, the apathy and selfishness of the relatives were deeply sickening, Sheila felt nauseated. She went back running to the changing room for nurses.

She kept sobbing for quite some time, she was the witness of the biggest healthcare failure of the century. All her education had failed in the face of this immense catastrophe. She had witnessed compassionate humanity at work when it came to the healthcare staff working and an epic of lack of concern from relatives of those who could not be saved. The relatives would fight savagely with the doctors and blame them of administering wrong treatment, neglecting their duties and mislabelling the bodies. No one bothered to check with the healthcare staff, what they were going through.

Sheila felt lost. She wanted to end her life at that point. Everything looked so dark. There appeared to be no hope for the future!

What was happening to her? An educated person was losing her emotional health and succumbing to pressures exhibited by the situation on her.

Emotional Health during Crisis:

Most common emotion during the crisis is anxiety. Anxiety disorder is an umbrella term that includes different conditions, the panic disorder being a significant one. During a panic, a person feels terror that strikes at random. During a panic attack, the person may also sweat, have chest pain, and feel palpitations (unusually strong or irregular heartbeats). Sometimes there is a feeling of choking or having a stroke.

During a crisis, people fall into patterns of behaviour they know that are not beneficial to them. OCD (obsessive compulsive disorder) makes the person experience severe anxiety and distress.

To relieve this anxiety, they perform some repetitive acts known as compulsions. Excessive cleanliness, repeated hand wash, obsession with orderliness, cleaning the house/kitchen, again and again, aligning the carpets/pillows/desktop, counting numbers, rechecking locked doors are typical OCD behaviors.

Emotional distress due to crisis may cause depression. A major depressive disorder is a common and serious medical illness that negatively affects how one feels, the way one thinks and how one acts. Feeling sad continually, loss of appetite, loss of purpose and sleep or too much sleeping, feeling worthless and suicidal thoughts (extreme cases), and lack of concentration are typical symptoms of depression. Many of us may feel sad at some point in time, but if the symptoms listed above linger with you for most of the day, you need professional help. Many people are not even aware that they are depressed!

Post-Traumatic Stress Disorder (PTSD) is a chronic psychiatric disorder that can occur in people who have experienced or witnessed a traumatic event, such as a serious accident, terrorist attack or a physical assault. In a worldwide crisis like Covid-19, it is not uncommon for people to recall and relive their earlier traumatic experiences and experience panic and numbness as a result of PTSD.

Social stigma in the context of health is the negative association between a person or group of people who share certain characteristics and a specific disease. In an outbreak, such as Covid-19, people infected with the virus may be labelled, stereotyped, discriminated against, treated separately, and/or experience loss of status because of a perceived link with a disease, or after returning home from quarantine. Stigma makes the person feel inferior and left out of society.

Anxiety, anger, depression, sadness, fatigue, fear, traumas - our list of emotional health issues seems to be ever-increasing. It is important to acknowledge them and deal with them.

Scene 3: Mona and Sandy fought again today. The swords of the words cut through their relationship which was already reeling under pressures of misunderstanding. Both of them have been working from home for the last four months and having to see each other 24x7 had put further strain on their relationship. Romance has vanished in thin air. Who would have believed they had a love marriage three years back?

Sandy got a pink slip from his company last week without the opportunity to serve a notice period. They were cutting down the workforce and he was among those who were summarily dismissed. It was in no way a reflection of his competence. The demand for the projects manufactured by his employer was so minimal that his private company was not in a position to retain the entire staff. The couple had a home loan and EMIs to pay. The bank had already served two reminders in the last 8 months for payment delays. Mona's salary was not much compared to Sandy's. They had a couple of months of credit card bills to pay as well.

The financial dent made both of them nervous. Due to the lockdown, they had no house help and had to manage things on their own. Both disliked domestic chores and would dispute about who should get up and open the door when the doorbell rang.

They had purchased the flat they currently occupied by paying a very steep price with the hope that Sandy would land an onsite deputation abroad. With Covid-19, countries had sealed their borders and all new work permits were denied. Consequently, Sandy's assignment got cancelled. Now, as Mona felt the heat of strained finances, love for her partner flew out of the window.

Sandy was already agonized at losing his job. He was also bored that he had only one human face to look at all day, and the face wore a permanently irritated look. Mona's rambling frustrated him even more. Earlier, he would have banged the door and left on his bike for a ride and some fresh air.

However, with the pandemic around, he had nowhere to go. Both husband and wife took to screaming at one another. Allegations flew like bullets in the air.

After half an hour after one such screaming match, Mona entered the kitchen to have a few glasses of water. She came back to the bedroom and handed a cup of coffee to Sandy. He hugged her. They sat there for some time, looking outside the window, supporting each other without any words. Both were clueless about what to do next.

This couple was reeling under pressure put on them by the external situation, losing power to that enemy. They were vulnerable, felt helpless with extreme disturbance in their emotional health due to social and financial crisis they were subjected to.

Health Psychology: Health is a state of complete physical, mental, and social well-being and not merely the absence of disease or infirmity, as per the WHO definition. Health psychology is a speciality that focuses on how biology, psychology, behaviour, and social factors influence health and illness. Health psychology emphasizes how behaviour influences health, it is uniquely positioned to help people change the behaviours that contribute to health and well-being.

The key approach used in health psychology is known as the 'biosocial model'. According to this view, illness and health are the results of a combination of biological (inherited personality traits and genetic conditions), psychological (personality characteristics, and stress levels), and social factors (support systems, family relationships, cultural beliefs).

Maintaining emotional health during a crisis:
Resilience is the capacity of a system, be it an individual, or an economy, to deal with change and continue to develop, even after a failure. Emotional health is a product of resilience and standing tall again after suffering a blow.

For maintaining emotional health, a person needs to become aware of his/her emotional state. If you are feeling a negative emotion, do not blame yourself, accept the emotion without judging it.

- Process the emotion and choose to respond rather than react. A reaction is a primal response. A response is an intelligently programmed reply.
- Stress can initiate the 'fight or flight' response, a complex reaction of neurologic and endocrinologic systems
- Good stress, called eustress, can be beneficial to you. Good stress can help with motivation, focus, energy, and performance
- Bad stress, called distress typically causes anxiety, concern, and a decrease in performance. It also feels uncomfortable, and it can lead to more serious issues if not addressed
- Choose to act within the circle of your bounds, do not get stressed for the things you cannot control
- Don't try to change others. Think and act about what you can do

Learned helplessness:
- Learned helplessness is a state that occurs after a person has experienced a stressful situation repeatedly.
- They come to believe that they are unable to control or change the situation, so they do not try, even when opportunities for change become available.
- Once a person having this experience discovers that they cannot control events around them, they lose motivation. Even if an opportunity arises that allows the person to alter their circumstances, they do not take action.
- They become passive in the face of trauma and allow an increase in stress levels

The 5-point formula:

- Become self-aware at every step and acknowledge your emotions. Do not discard anything, even the seemingly negative emotions.
- Accept yourself and others with an open heart. Be kind and allow for occasional slips. The world is not perfect, neither are you!
- Be driven by a purpose in life. Your purpose should be so big that it makes you take your mind off your emotional turbulences.
- Create moments of serenity for yourself. Make space for discreet 'me time' moments of happiness. Such moments can create wonders in your life.
- Be the master of your emotions by improving the quality of your self-talk. Count your blessings, and remind yourself that you can sail through the distress.

Being emotionally healthy does not mean lack of emotions. It just means that you can process them better to become lucky in life.

So be happy! Be physically fit and emotionally healthy! And enjoy life.
You are worth it!

Abha Jadhav

is a passionate and affectionate educator with an experience of over two decades in her chosen field. She is currently the principal of the Apex International School, Surat. She has not only been able to nurture her students academically but also inculcate essential values and life skills in them with her energy, enthusiasm and vivaciousness. She is a recipient of the *Star Employee of the Year* and *Dronacharya* awards. She has been nominated for the *Best Principal Award* for two consecutive years.

Abha is a certified trainer and parenting coach. She has been counselling parents for over a decade now. Her '3D approach' has been lauded by parents for making their parenting skills more effective and graceful.

As a highly successful insurance agent, she has won most of the well-known awards in the industry.

Abha was one of the top five finalists of *Mrs. Gujarat Beauty Pageant* in 2007. She is a popular radio and television host. She also hosts her own YouTube talk show *Spotlight with Abha*.

Abha has a unique ability to spread smiles and transfer her positivity to people she connects with.

2. Emotional mastery

By Abha Jadhav

Life is short, live it. Love is rare, grab it. Anger is bad, dump it. Fear is awful, face it. Memories are sweet, cherish them.

Unknown

It was a beautiful March morning. Spring winds were pampering Asmi's cheeks. She was deep in thought as she was expecting her reports, which would either illuminate her life with happiness or shatter her dreams. Even after eight years of their marriage, Asmi and her husband Aarav, were childless. After many treatments, today there was hope. Finally, the news that they were waiting for came through. Asmi called Aarav to share the good news. Aarav rushed back from office and lifted Asmi in his arms with joy on hearing what they were waiting to hear for long.

But the happiness didn't last long. About two months later, Asmi suffered a miscarriage. Both Asmi and Aarav were shattered as if their most precious gem has been stolen. Asmi went into depression. The smile on her face was replaced with sadness. Her mother-in-law began ill-treating her and even labelled her 'unlucky'. She began to harass Asmi and call her all sorts of names. Even Aarav began ignoring her. Instead of being her strongest support at a time like this, he kept away from her. Asmi was not allowed to visit her parents either. She felt suffocated and wanted to find someone with whom she could share her pain but she was totally alone. In disgust, she overdosed on sleeping pills one day. Luckily, Aarav took her to the hospital in time and she was saved. Shockingly, her husband and mother-in-law did not inform her parents of the incident.

Aarav and his mother were terrified of being hauled into a police station for subjecting Asmi to domestic violence. They were afraid of going to jail because of Asmi's attempt to commit suicide.

They sent her to her maternal place who pretended that it would give her some rest. Three months later, she was served a divorce notice by Aarav. For Asmi who was already going through a lot of pain, this was like the proverbial last nail in her coffin of pain.

It took over one year for Asmi to get a handle on what was happening. She realised that the plea of Aarav and his family not wanting to be accused of domestic violence because of her attempt to suicide was just a cover up. The reality was that Aarav was having an affair with another girl. This prompted Asmi to agree to the divorce. Aarav was so heartless, that he asked the judge to give the decree in a week as he was getting married again.

This hit Asmi hard. She felt as if she was being sucked into a quagmire.

Six months passed by following the separation. She spent most of her time confined to her room and wept the whole day. One day, her brother advised her to take up a job to stay busy. It would help her divert her pain. Unwillingly, Asmi agreed. Through some recommendations, she got an offer to teach in a school. But, in a weeks' time she ran out of confidence realising that she was not set out to be a teacher. She walked into the principal's room and announced that she did not wish to continue. Though the principal empathised with Asmi, she asked her to work till they found a new teacher.

Though reluctant to prolong what was not a pleasant experience for her, she agreed.

In the next one month, she surprised everyone with her enthusiasm and the way she worked with her class. She forgot that she had submitted her resignation. She got engrossed in teaching and pouring love and affection on the kids. She had found what was lacking in her life. But it was not easy to work with a boss who knew that you have been appointed with a recommendation. The principal often asked Asmi to carry out personal errands for her.

In disgust, Asmi resigned and left.

She got a job in another school. This time, without any recommendation. With her dedication and sincerity towards her profession and her caring nature towards the children, she soon became the apple of everyone's eyes. She was known for her smile and energy. Three years passed happily.

Destiny, however, had fresh plans in store for Asmi.

Ms. Verma, a shrewd and rude lady with a horrible dressing sense, who had earned the dubious distinction of disturbing the peace among the teachers. As luck would have it, Ms, Verma was appointed principal of the school. This led to another turn in Asmi's Life. One day, she called Asmi and asked her to become her informer. Though stunned, she refused politely. She was called again with the same request. On both occasions, she refused to have any part to play in the matter. The principal started harassing her under various pretexts. She went to the extent of levelling false allegations against her. Asmi, who was already under a lot of stress, resigned and left the school. It was a difficult decision to take, as she was single, living alone and had no other source of income.

For three months Asmi was jobless. She had no money to even pay her landlord. But as they say, God helps those who are ready to face challenges. She got a job in a bigger and more reputed institution than the one she had resigned from. Though challenging at first, she spared no pains to give her best. Soon, she earned the reputation of being one of the best teachers among the students and parents.

However, all workplaces come with their own share of challenges. Some people who knew that Asmi was a divorcee, and tried to play with her emotions. They started to keep away from her. Some others even avoided talking to her. Some good teachers stood by her and this gave her strength to weather the storm. The students too loved Asmi, and this sustained her passion to keep giving value.

She never looked back and continued to shower her love on her students, which inculcated values in her students while contributing to their academic growth.

Six happy years passed by. Asmi was quite satisfied with her work and also with the people around her. She had won everyone's heart with her hard work and passion for her subject. No one could find a fault with her work. She had turned into a perfectionist. She also worked for three direct marketing companies and won accolades everywhere.

All along, Asmi continued to upgrade her qualifications and skills. She, in fact, turned into a newer better version of herself. This was then she decided to shift to a bigger school, which had a corporate style of functioning. However, fresh challenges awaited her. She made new friends and also got a mentor to guide her. She radiated an aura that was contributing to her gradual rise at work. Her success also attracted the jealously of some of her colleagues who envied her popularity among the students.

One day, while teaching in a class, she inadvertently blurted out something about a teacher named Binita and regretted it instantly. Alas! Words once spoken cannot be taken back. The matter reached Binita who was understandably furious. The issue caught steam and the matter reached the principal. It took a lot of effort on Asmi's part to correct the situation. She not only apologized in front of everyone but tried to regain her friendship with Binita. In fact, once when Binita wanted to shift her seat from where she used to sit earlier near Asmi, no one welcomed her. Finally, when Binita was complaining about this with tears in her eyes, Asmi approached Binita silently and kept her bag at her old place. Asmi even told her that she would not sit beside her if Binita has a problem, and requested her not to change her seat. Binita was shocked. Next day, she called Asmi and welcomed her with a smile, and said, "When I described the whole incident to my mother, she made me understand that you are actually my real friend. Let us be friends again."

The two women became good friends thereafter.

Asmi went on to work at a few other institutions and became better with every passing day. She heads an institution now. She is satisfied with her life. But her thirst for knowledge and the desire to share it with her students blazes even more fiercely than it ever has. She is loved by her students and her teachers as well.

Lessons from Asmi's life

Never underestimate yourself: Asmi's Life was full of turbulence but she never gave up. She never quit and never lost hope. She overcame her depression and gave herself another chance to look at her life with a new perspective. She discovered that there was a treasure of hidden talents inside her, which got wings when she entered a job. Never underestimate yourself when life throws up some unexpected challenges. What would have happened to Asmi's career if she had left teaching immediately in her very first job. She found her happiness in the smiles of young kids, which nurtured her motherhood. It filled that vacant place of child in her Life. And so, when she started giving her love and care along with the teaching, she flourished in her career.

Working with depression

How can one work with depression? If you keep depression aside and do not fall back into remembrance mode every now and then, it will become easy to work even if you are suffering from depression. Depression is only a mental condition where a person is going through some kind of traumatic situation, where his feelings are not under his control. If a person decides to cocoon himself in his or her sad, depressive feelings, it becomes difficult to progress. It is important therefore to shed the sadness and fear of being alone and see the abundant happiness, colours, and success.

Asmi's went through the trauma of losing a baby, a broken marriage, and living Life all alone. If she had married again, could she have led a settled life? Maybe, or maybe not. But she was determined to prove to the world that she could lead her life on her own terms. She decided to shed her depression, pain, and loneliness and made up her mind to face the world by distributing smiles and happiness to others. She not only won over her depression but also helped others to be happy and cheerful.

Life doesn't end with the end of a relationship or rejection of people. Actually, a new life is born. Leave those people behind who say 'log kya kahenge'. Live your life king size.

Walk in other's shoes

When you see someone going through an emotional trauma, put yourself in their place instead of mocking them. It is easy to criticize and comment unthinkingly but have you ever considered what you would have done if you had been in her place?

Asmi's colleagues did not allow her to be a part of their get-togethers, thinking of the backlash from their friends and relatives for inviting a divorcee. It was for this reason that in her second job, Asmi pretended that she was a married woman and told everyone that her husband was abroad. Though it was tough to live a false life, it was done to save herself from social stigma. When she started wearing the symbols of a married woman, she was heartily welcomed by her colleagues.

A very important lesson is that, when you are at your workplace, be professional and do not bother about someone's personal life. Once you stop peeping in the personal lives of others, your professional relations improve automatically. It is not difficult at all.

Please keep talking

When I say 'talk', I don't mean chit-chatting in office during work hours. What I mean is that it is important to keep communication channels open. Whenever you have any doubt or questions about any colleague, talk to them about what you have heard or something that is bothering you about that person.

Remember, the incident between Asmi and Binita? If Binita had approached Asmi immediately after knowing what has been said in the session, the matter could have been resolved easily without the very public fireworks. We should never forget that most difficult issues can be resolved over a coffee table.

Such conversations must be done face-to-face rather than over the telephone. When you talk face-to-face, it becomes easy to grasp what another person has gone through. Therefore, never hesitate to talk. No matter how serious the issue is. Silence kills the possibility of a solution in such cases.

It is possible that the colleague whom you want to talk to is not ready to respond. In such case, take help of a common friend. When you meet, keep calm, take a deep breath, and start your conversation on a positive note. This will help you calm down your colleague if he is furious. In most cases, communication helps one resolve glitches among colleagues.

It is also important to ensure that you remain non-judgemental in your conversations in your workplace. This is the right thing to do because you do not even know your colleagues properly. By the time you realise and apologize for your judgment, it could be too late. It is very easy to make fun of a colleague at your workplace but it is very difficult to mend fences and repair a relationship once it is fractured by casually spoken words uttered without thinking.

Whenever, you get stuck or miss out any opportunity because of the actions of a subordinate, senior or colleague, you feel angry. The temptation to react to the slight by raising your voice is very strong.

Don't! Never react instantly or take a decision when you are angry. In anger, we often use unpleasant language and take hasty decisions that we regret later. Whenever you feel that you are going to get angry, drink a glass of water, keep calm, take 10 deep breaths slowly. Decide your next action only when you are calm.

To keep your aggression under control, be aware of what triggers you, and what makes you fly into a rage. Keep away from such triggers. Do not let others know what makes you furious in your workplace. Your rivals or competitors may use your anger against you.

Apologize easily

There is nothing wrong in apologising if you know that you have hurt someone or done something wrong to someone. An apology from your side mends relations and often improves inter-personal bonding and team performance. Remember, the one who initiates an apology, always adds value to his own character. People at work are certain to appreciate your humble and down to earth nature.

Let us recall the words Asmi, uttered about Binita. She realized and waited for Binita to come and talk. Till then, the matter had worsened. Asmi, sent her apology in a message to Binita and even apologized in front of whole staff, which ultimately made her popular because everyone considered her a humble person.

Work is for office

When you leave for home, leave your work pressure, aggression, tension behind. Go home with a smile, and relaxed mood. After all, it is for the happiness of your family that you are working so hard. Whenever you return home in the evening and your wife opens the door for you, give her a smile of satisfaction so she knows everything is well. Playing with your children, talking with your parents, helping your wife in the kitchen will rejuvenate and recharge you with a new energy to start your next day at office, and help your performance reach magical heights.

Suffocated at work?

It may happen that after working for a long time, some people may start taking you for granted. Some new employees may make you feel outdated and you could start feeling suffocated in the organisation for which you have worked with dedication for many years. When you feel suffocated and cannot think of a way to go ahead, take a step back, analyse the way you have been working. Identify the room for improvement and keep updating yourself constantly. Take help of a good friend, who knows and understands you well. Enrol yourself for some professional courses to upgrade yourself. And if you still feel nothing is working, it makes sense to start looking for a new job.

Our life is a tidal wave of crests and troughs in the ocean of emotions. You have to ensure that you sail safely, by handling your emotions well. If you can do this, you are likely to reach the pinnacle of both personal and professional success with relative ease.

It's time to rise from failures, and learn lessons from them instead of getting disappointed and depressed. Find out the reasons you failed to handle your emotions, and work on it.

Ajay Ugalmugle

is an HR professional who has served with distinction in the
public sector as well with multinational corporations for a quarter
of a century in diverse fields ranging from engineering to
technology and from chemicals to pharmaceuticals.

He has hands-on experience of setting up of a greenfield
project and of business closure and restructuring. His
achievements include the functional integration of several newly-
acquired businesses into parent organizations.

Driven by the intent of sharing his knowledge of Labour Law
compliance and providing assistance in the creation of a
professional HR set-up for clients in the MSME industry, Ajay
established his firm *Auxilium HR* in 2015.

He is a corporate trainer specializing in Labour Law.
Ajay is considered an influential voice in the fields of HR and IR
and is highly respected for his inisghts into labour law and
statutory compliance.

3. My adventures with life and labor law training

By Ajay Ugalmugle

Stand up, be bold, be strong. All the strength and succor you need is within yourself. Therefore, make your own future

Swami Vivekananda

When I look back at how far I have come from the days of my school, and what I have achieved, I find my journey to be satisfying in many ways. Socially, I was and still am an introvert, especially when I am in the company of strangers, and yet I have changed too. During school days, I was more focused on games and sports and not enough on my studies, though I did manage to score a first-class in my SSC exams. This was a fairly decent accomplishment in the late 70s. I graduated in science and went on to pursue my master's in Personnel Management. I hardly understood what Personnel Management was. I nevertheless took the path on the advice of a close relative. It was a proud feeling to be a student of management studies, which kindled in me the hope of making it big in the future. There was a sense of uncertainty about the opportunities that awaited me and the competition I would have to face.

After completing the fourth semester, I got myself enrolled in a placement agency. There were no computers back then and very few phones.

The first interaction with the director of the placement agency was very discouraging. He shot some questions from my management textbooks at me. Though I had cleared the first three semesters with good marks and had the confidence to clear the fourth as well, I was not able to answer many of the questions to his satisfaction. He called me each Sunday to his office and fired a fresh volley of questions at me.

More than the preparations for my exams, I gained a better understanding of the subject with this exercise with each passing Sunday. This helped me groom myself to face an interview. After six months of scouting, I was hired by one of India's giant public sector companies. After spending more than seven years in the company, I resigned from my position for exploring avenues that would challenge me and help me learn more.

To sum up my corporate experience, I consider myself fortunate to have gotten the right breaks at the right time. In my 27 years of corporate experience, I had the opportunity to work in a Greenfield project, to negotiate the shutting down of a factory with a vociferous union, and negotiating an amicable settlement. I was also part of a merger and acquisition team that successfully integrated two companies. Having worked with different companies in diverse situations, I enhanced my working understanding of labor laws.

Beginning of 2015, I came out of corporate service to pursue my HR career independently. I started an HR consultancy firm with an objective to provide end to end HR services to corporates. Training being one of our verticals. In March 2015, I landed an assignment with a company for conducting an open training session on Labor Laws as a freelancer, to be held in the second week of June 2015. Initially I was nervous to accept the assignment as I had never conducted a professional training but managed to gather the courage to accept the offer. I started my preparations by structuring my knowledge in a presentation form. As the days passed, the training slides started taking shape. However, I began getting progressively more nervous, so much so that, I hoped that the training would get canceled for some reason. Three days before the actual training, all my expectations were quashed. I received confirmation that there are sufficient nominations, and the training would be held as scheduled. I also received the list of participants with the name of the companies they were from and their designations. Most of the participants were senior professionals in HR with over 15 to 20 years in their line of work. The list added to my anxiety. Let me recount a few thoughts that entered my mind:

Why would these co-professionals with so many years of experience behind them want to listen to me?

What difference can I make to their knowledge?

Can I add value in any way to them?

As a result, will I be able to deliver my topic with confidence?

If I ran my presentation, and explained each slide, without the session getting interactive, I would complete the topic by lunchtime.

How do I manage post-lunch session in such a scenario?

The day arrived. I drove to the venue and reached half an hour before the time of commencement of the scheduled training. I connected my laptop to the projector and waited for the participants to trickle in. Some of them had serious faces and grey hair, which appeared to agitate the butterflies in my stomach even more. The session was to start at 10 AM but a few participants were late and the organizer requested me to wait for them to reach.

The program started at 10.30 AM.

After a brief introduction by the organizer, I took to the stage and introduced myself in some detail. I elaborated on my achievements in different companies after which I asked participants to introduce themselves and share their purpose of attending this program. The advantage of this exercise was that it not only gave me some more time to douse my nervousness but also allowed me to understand what the participants were expecting from the session.

I started with my first slide. After touching upon the introduction on National Labour Policy, the different legislations, and their categorization, I went on to the first legislation of the presentation - PF Act 1952.

It was also the law about which most participants were keen to know more given the amendments that had been made recently and also due to changes in a few operating processes caused by ongoing digitalization. Within a few minutes, I started getting questions on the subject. Answering them helped me shake away my initial nervousness. I answered and encouraged participants to ask more questions. My ability to give satisfactory answers helped me build my confidence, as I realized that the attendees were not only listening to me, but also keen on knowing more.

By the time I was done shedding light on the first topic, it was lunchtime. Two hours from the commencement of the program, I sensed that I was a different person. I had gained all the confidence I required. I was being looked at with respect as someone with answers. I was gaining fluency in delivering my talk. Even today, I experience more fluency when I am conducting trainings as compared to my normal conversations.

Post-lunch, the context of my nervousness shifted. I was nervous, whether I would be able to wrap-up the program within the scheduled closing time of 5.30 PM as I had to deliver a few more topics. Interestingly, post-lunch the attention of the participants was more sustained, and they were interacting with enthusiasm, which was very encouraging due to which the session got extended by an hour. All the participants continued to stay put and their intense involvement did not flag. My throat went sore speaking the whole day and my legs pained from standing but I felt a great sense of achievement washing over me at the end of the day. As the program ended, the participants stood-up and applauded, thanking me for the knowledge they had gained during the day's process. Such a gesture is unusual in programs of such nature. It was indeed a memorable experience. I discovered a new me that evening.

By the end of that day, my journey as a trainer had begun.

Later, as I wondered what value I added to the lives of those participants, I realized that more than the subject knowledge, it was the sharing of the practical experiences which I had encountered during my corporate career that had appealed to them the most. Making them realize the key importance of the minute things that are routinely ignored made all the difference. It was the extra 15-20% of information that added value to my program.

Of all the subjects, I chose Labour Law as my topic because no business can exist without adhering to Labour Laws. All small or big businesses must comply with its stipulations.

Ignorance of the law is not an excuse entertained by any governing authority. Therefore, training on the subject becomes that much more significant for professionals responsible for compliance of law in the organization. It is similar in sports too, where players have to adhere to all applicable rules and regulations. Imagine what would happen to the games we play, if there were no rules. Even a board game played within the four walls of our home, with our family members is played according to the rules of that game. We experience displeasure at some point if one of the members flout a rule. Displeasure turns into anger and often leads to abrupt abandonment of the game.

A business is no exception.

Labour laws are enacted by the Government to offer economic and social justice to industrial employees. Generally, these laws provide guidelines to the employers/industrialists in dealing with the matters of wages, working hours and the working conditions of labor. All laws have been enacted with a very specific purpose.

Let's consider some examples.

The Payment of Wages Act: This act was passed to regulate the timely payment of wages and to ensure that there are no unauthorized deductions. It is to protect the employees from exploitation, especially employees in the low salary bracket. If employees are being paid their monthly salary latest by the seventh day of the following month, it is due to the fact that the employer is bound by law to do so. In absence of such a law, employers would have used their discretion to decide when the payment has to be made, largely to their convenience.

The Maternity Benefit Act: The objective of the Act is to protect the dignity of motherhood and the dignity of a new person's birth by providing for the full and healthy maintenance of the woman and her child at this important time when she is not working.

This act compels the employer to provide maternity benefits to female employees. In the absence of a law, would such a benefit have been possible?

The PF Act: This act provides provision for the post-retirement phase of an employee's life by making the saving's under the law mandatory

Similarly there are other laws which carry a meaningful purpose in the interest of the employees as well as the employers.

Many employers lack knowledge on labour laws. In the absence of knowledge, they err in its implementation and attract punitive legal action, which causes business disruption. Labour laws give structure to the workplace and define the obligations of employees and employers towards each other. The laws provides the necessary direction to both parties in resolving workplace conflict.

It is also to be noted that these laws are dynamic. The legislation keeps on getting amended as per the changing situations and needs and hence it becomes essential for the businesses to keep themselves abreast with updated labor laws.

Hence, the role of a trainer becomes that more important.

Looking at my journey so far, I have realized how important it is to overcome inhibitions and stand-up to your intent. Through these trainings I have derived great satisfaction and sense of responsibility for creating awareness on a subject which is an integral part of business. Teaching is always a unique opportunity to learn as well as give back.

On the personal front, my journey as a trainer has helped me explore a different side of my personality which has been an altogether new experience.

Ananya Nori

is a Tsunami survivor, Mindfulness and Meditation Coach, A Resilience coach, a certified Neuro-Linguistic Programming (NLP) practitioner. She is a corporate thought leader with close to two decades in Banking, Telecommunications, Healthcare, HR, and Project Management.

She is on a mission to provide what she calls 1% mindfulness to corporate professionals by using her knowledge of NLP to transform their lives and careers. She is also the Founder of the **3R Framework Course** to transform individuals, which she developed using NLP techniques and her own experiences during her eight-year-long transformational journey.

She is the Founder of the ***Resilience Revolution – The Silent Evolution Talk Show*** on YouTube, which encourages professionals to build resilience within themselves and their lives as a critical ingredient of success.

Ananya Nori is a co-author of the book *Being Employable,* a collaborative work initiated by Jogesh Jain on behalf of JJ School of Employability. This article is a tribute to all her Gurus.

4. NOW!

By Ananya Nori

Mindfulness has the great power to heal, recharge, and transform our inner beings, relationships, and work.
Mindfulness helps you fall in love with the ordinary.

Thich Nhat Hanh

Mindfulness is the quality or state of being conscious or aware of something. It is a mental state achieved by focusing one's awareness on the present moment, while calmly acknowledging and accepting one's feelings, thoughts, and bodily sensations, used as a therapeutic technique.

My First Experience of Mindfulness

I survived the tsunami by becoming mindful that something massive would happen at the time, and I was able to save myself and my friend (who is my husband now) who accompanied me. Though it was not a pleasant experience, and I was disturbed, mindfulness made me aware of the moment and the environment around me. I was able to heed my inner voice and save both of us, narrowly escaping death by a few seconds. I wasn't aware that it was mindfulness that had helped me. It was in 2012-2013, eight years after the incident, that I realized what had made me act in the nick of time.

I wrote a poem on the Tsunami experience:

Tsunami
On a lovely Sunday Morning;
On the shore at a distance while sauntering!
Slowly saw a wave once hit my feet,
Took it lightly, couldn't strike a meaning underneath.

A few seconds later, the second wave hit me.
Realized you whispered; something's wrong,
The first time felt thy presence!
Life changed for me ever since!

From near the water, we had only two minutes,
People around, watching and laughing;
I knew I could run, only Relay;
We made it, for, upon thee, I rely.

30 feet high; a sudden gush of water,
What an escape!! For a beautiful reason!
A nightmare for two years! "Tsunami" is its name!
Is there a person who caught "You"; without Fame?

From tears of troubles to tears of bliss;
At every turn, it used to be a roller-coaster
You waited until I had to surrender!
In the end, "You" proved what "You" could render!

5 Busting Myths of Mindfulness

What I learned about the power of mindfulness in the years
that followed; could fill the pages of a book. For now, I shall limit
myself to busting some common myths on the subject.

- **Mindfulness is not a quick fix:** It takes time and practice
  to be truly mindful. We need to be patient and trust the
  process as we unlearn patterns acquired over a lifetime.
- **Mindfulness is not a miracle cure:** Do not expect stress to
  disappear when we are mindful magically. We can change
  the way we look at our past through the daily practice of
  meditation
- **Mindfulness is not trying to empty our mind of
  conscious thought:** We learn instead to observe our

thoughts and thought patterns and respond to them with greater accuracy.

- **Some minds are too busy to meditate:** The function of the brain is to keep the mind occupied with constant thought. The mindfulness practice is something we must learn to imbibe to break the patterns easily. We also would be able to learn, to let go of the numerous thoughts, and thus bring the mind to the present moment.

- **You don't stop planning for the future:** It is not that we stop focusing on the future but pay attention to our experiences in the present moment. We can't change the past experiences we have had; however, the future can be determined by what we choose to do now.

Ways to Mindfulness Practice

Food

Food, in my opinion, is an important area that one should be mindful about; Sadhguru Jaggi Vasudev, in his discourses, reveals that many monks and seers in the past insisted that we eat mindfully. The food that we eat should make us agile and alert.

In the book *Inner Engineering − A yogi's guide to joy*, Sadhguru states, "We need to experiment with various food, cooked meat, raw food. We should not ask doctors or anyone what food is suitable for us, rather observe how each food influences us. Food, water, and the air; we see them as commodities and not as "life-making materials."

Our ancestors laid out a process while eating; they said that we have to eat slowly and only 24 morsels of food in one meal, as it would keep us mindful. Sadhguru also explains in detail why vegetarian food is a better fit for humans. He underlines the consequences of eating both cooked meat and vegetables.

I am still experimenting, but I have identified foods that do not allow me to be agile and alert - like bread, buns, and pizzas.

Certain foods keep me light and nimble like chapatis, fruits, and porridges. If I eat late at night, I eat very little. If I eat early evening, I eat a full meal that fills my stomach 80 percent as prescribed in the lovely book – *Ikigai – The Japanese Secret to a Long and Happy Life by Hector Garcia and Francesc Miralles*. I try to keep myself alert and mindful as I eat.

Water:

Seventy percent of our body is water. We must observe how water influences us. Drinking water from a copper vessel can do wonders, as I experience every day. One day I went to a relative's house with my brother to invite them to his wedding. They served us water since we did not want coffee.

"It tastes *sweet," I shouted with excitement.*

My brother, who was drinking the same water, did not notice anything unusual in the taste. He was perplexed; I recalled another instance when the water had tasted sweet. I asked the hosts if they had stored water in a copper vessel. The lady confirmed that the water did come from a copper vessel, as I had pointed out. There are several health benefits of drinking water stored in a copper vessel, as described in our ancient scriptures.

Ninety-three-year-old monk Thich Nhat Hanh is another teacher whom I follow. He is a classic example of mindfulness practice and teaching. Hahn talks about being mindful as a way of life and not as a specialized practice. He says, "The energy of mindfulness helps us touch life deeply throughout the day, whether we're brushing our teeth, washing the dishes, walking to work, eating a meal, or driving the car. We can be mindful while standing, walking, or lying down; while speaking, listening, working, playing, and cooking."

Cool, isn't it?

It is indeed possible with immense practice. Have I mastered it all? No! I have a lot to learn! When I first learned that it is possible to be mindful even when we perform our daily tasks, I was amazed.

"How can one exercise awareness during the performance of what one considers mundane chores?" I soon learned that if I am not mindful, even properly cooking a meal becomes a challenge and, I end up messing the dishes I prepare!

Becoming more mindful

There are various practices laid out to us by our ancestors. Have you ever tried lighting a lamp or a candle with a match stick? What do we do to light it? We have to ensure that the wind doesn't snuff the fire on the match stick before lighting the lamp or the candle. This simple act makes us mindful. It brings us to the present. If we are not careful, we could end up with burned fingers. It is a simple but potent act. You may want to try it out if you have not done so yet.

Ekart Tolle, in his book *The Power of Now*, describes the esoteric meaning of waiting. Jesus also has used the analogy of waiting in some of his parables. It is not about restless waiting that denies the present moment it's due and expects the future to be perfect. It is about the moment of waiting in absolute stillness, where we are fully awake and alert. It was the silence that had descended upon me as I sat on the beach before the tsunami struck. Even though drenched in my thoughts thoroughly, I became utterly aware of the present.

The "waiting" Jesus talks about that you are likely to miss out if you are not completely awake, alert, or aware of the present moment. There is no fear in such awaiting, just a mindful presence. "Be like a servant waiting for the return of the master," says Jesus.

The servant may not know when the master would arrive. He is therefore expected to be in a state of constant alertness, poised, awake, and still. He wouldn't get caught off-guard when his master arrives.

RISE AND SHINE

Whenever we are waiting, wherever it may be, we may use the time to observe the bodily sensations. Even if we stand in long queues or find ourselves stuck in traffic jams, we can choose to enjoy the moments instead of being worried or anxious. Unless we stay in the present, our mind will take over and be continuously controlled by it. We get caught up with the mind-controlling us, and we fail to remain in the present; we, therefore, become anxious and lose our happiness forever.

To develop the observation of bodily sensations, Yoga comes handy in a huge way. When we practice Yoga, every move we take needs mindfulness. We need to do everything slowly and mindfully. As we do it every day, we gradually become mindful. We also have advanced Yogic Practices, where we become aware of the energy that moves within us. It can be a bit strenuous, but if we cultivate a conducive environment and consume an appropriate diet. In this inner energy body, our vital energies' dance becomes a matter of our conscious experience.

Isha Hatha Yoga and Art of living are two different Yoga teaching centers I have learned from and experienced. As Sadhguru states, doing Yoga, the bookish way is not right. Widely taught is the Patanjali Yoga sutra. My school teachers taught me Yoga from the book. It did help me exercise, but the Yoga I learned from the Art of Living and the Isha Yoga center benefitted me in many more ways. My focus has improved; I can sense and identify myself with my bodily sensations when I focus. Though I fail to notice the inflow and outflow of my breath every moment, in a deep meditative state, I do sense the energy movement within the body.

Saint Agastya made Yoga simple for villagers when he scaled the Vindhyas and came to the South. He wove it into everyday life in a manner that it became a part of the culture and not a system of exercises that one has to make time and space. Generations after generations passed the simple yogic poses until they have reached us.

The way we sit on the ground to eat, the famous crossed-legged posture is considered a powerful pose in which every villager settles. As he or she squats to sit is also a powerful pose in the Yogic tradition for many reasons.

We must incorporate these traditions that nourish mindfulness in our daily lives and pass it on to the upcoming generations. It is a debt we owe to our ancestors. It is a gift indented for the forthcoming generations.

Let us be worthy guardians of this powerful flame.

Pallavi Rane

is a social development professional and certified trainer with a master's degrees in social work, and an MBA in social entrepreneurship. She works with NGOs, corporate entities, government institutions, international organizations, and factories. This unique blend of qualifications and professional exposure enables her understanding of varied perspectives and expectations of different types of institutions and stakeholders.

Pallavi possesses comprehensive knowledge of CSR-Sustainability rules as well as wide-ranging practical experience in the area of implementation of CSR programs. She has a deep understanding of NGO laws and their functionality. She is aware of the 'due diligence process' of selecting NGOs for a project. She has implemented CSR projects across the different states of India, and has worked on international projects as well.

Pallavi has been appreciated by her clients for her ability to encourage teams and explain difficult concepts through effective training methodologies and experiential learning approaches. She has been able to show proven tangible improvement in people's performance through effective interventions to over 2000 participants. Pallavi is guest lecture faculty at SNDT Women's University, Churchgate and Nirmala Niketan, Mumbai.

5. Study that case, play that role

By Pallavi Rane

An organization's ability to learn, and translate that learning into action rapidly, is the ultimate competitive advantage.

Jack Welch
Former General Electric CEO

Farmer Company Limited (FCL) is a private limited company incorporated under the Companies Act, 1956. FCL is one of the largest and most diversified suppliers of sustainable fruits in India and has a strong commitment to organic farming. Working with almost 87,000 farmers sustainably cultivating fruits using certified processes, FCL offers a range of high-quality fruits to meet the needs of the customers.

FCL approached the trainer to build the capacity of its Field Workers (FW) on good farming principles/criteria and make employees more receptive to online training courses/ modules.

The problem definition-I

The trainer's first course of action was to know the FWs of FCL and understand their existing knowledge of farming principles/criteria. This was achieved through detailed one-on-one interviews with employees and FWs. When the FWs conducted sessions with a group of farmers under the trainer's supervision, the following problems were identified:

- The major role of the FW's is to collect initial and field diary data of farmers, gather the farmers for village level meetings, coordinate internal and external assessments by a third party and contact individual farmers for sessions and follow-up. However, in reality, the farmer group meetings were managed and sometimes conducted by the manager. Thus the roles and responsibilities of managers have increased, keeping them heavily occupied during the farming season.

- This has also reduced the public speaking confidence of the FW's. They are neither trained nor expected to conduct the meetings. During the field visits, it was observed that even the best of the FW's could not address the farmers as a group, failing which the adoption of the learnings and the objective of farmer training was lost.
- There were critical issues in the message delivery. The farmers had a casual attitude towards learning anything new. They were non-cooperative. There was a top-down approach in information dissemination leading to communication breakdown as farmers vehemently kept presenting their problems rather than exploring solutions. During the discussions, FW's passions surfaced and their inabilities to convey messages successfully led to frustration.
- There was a trust issue between farmers and staff therefore the casual attitude towards FW's and their messages.
- Farmers were aware that the knowledge of FWs was inadequate as they failed to address their queries and offer solutions or alternatives to their customary practices. As a result, they made fun of the FWs who repeated the sessions every year without actually addressing their concerns.
- The incompetency of FWs was a result of their poor knowledge with regards to agronomy as they were not qualified in the said field.
- FW's sessions with the farmers are monotonous and mechanical. There is no two-way participation and communication at all.

The problem definition-II

Besides, the FCL management team also discussed online training courses/modules with the trainer. The trainers were of the opinion that the employees were attuned to classroom training and were resistant to new changes like the introduction of online training. This has caused reduction in work productivity, and resulted in increasing requests for transfers, grumbling, hostility and the expression of a number of pseudo-logical reasons why the change and the online training would not work.

After getting a comprehensive view from the management, the trainer had a discussion with the employees on implementing 'online training'. The response was not supportive. The employees were agitated and constantly grumbling about the new changes being made.

FCL management expectations

- The management expected the trainers to help the team of FWs by improvising their communication and interpersonal skills and ensuring percolation of the updated knowledge to farmers and their families. Thereby, FCL could attract more farmers to join the programme. As a result, FCL could get quality products to sell to their customers and avail compliance certification.
- FCL management expected their employees to be trained using online training method. However, there was resistance to change, which affected the output. Management believed that a change in 'mind-set' of the employees towards online training would help FCL to curtail their expenses incurred on off-line training, as well as employee learning, which could be tracked by the management. This would improve the performance and productivity of the employees and organisation.

The trainer's approach

- The trainer decided to incorporate all the challenges observed by the team while designing the training intervention. They planned to use the skills and strengths of the team to demonstrate how the challenges can be easily managed. The idea was to offer simple steps to slightly alter the current methods being used.
- 'Learning by doing' approach was selected with actual situations of concern in focus. The idea was to do things differently and creatively so that the outcomes would be evident both in the classroom training sessions as well as during tests out in the field.

Why role play?

To address the training needs and incorporate the 'learning by doing' approach the trainer decided to adopt role play and case study methods. Role Play would help the trainees prepare for training sessions and overcome nervousness, anxiety and boost their confidence. The trainer aimed to prepare the trainees for difficult conversations and situations.

To accomplish the objective learning planning, meeting preparation, communication skills, presentation and how to hold a meeting, a practical field situation was created. Few volunteers were selected to enact the roles of farmers, family and field force workers. FW got dressed up in costumes and practiced. The role play was guided by the trainer. The trainer assigned home assignments to the trainees as the training was residential. Box 1 describes the role play scenarios.

Box 1: Role play scenarios

Scenario 1: Trainers took the example from farming principle/criteria i.e. to convince the farmer to do a soil test and submit a test report to the government laboratory. A role-playing exercise patterned around the farm flex, which trainer got along with them at the training venue. Out of the total 35 FWs, 5 of them acted as farmers, 2 of them became farmer's wives (as they also contribute to the farm), 2 were children and 1 of them was the FW. The rest the FWs were asked to observe and make notes.

Scene 1- It was seen in the role play that the FW is preparing himself for the farmer meeting. He is referring to his training notes and while accessing more information on the internet where he finds a video on soil testing. The FW makes a phone call to the farmer to inform him that he will be reaching the village in half an hour. The appearance of the FW was has shown to be happy, positive, and confident. The FW reaches the meeting spot at the committed time and farmers are also present right on time. Instead of directly initiating the session, the FW inquires about the previous year's farm season, about their children's schooling and the price rate at which they sold fruits. By doing this, the FW tries to build rapport before he begins with his technical session. In addition to rapport building, he also explains about some government schemes to the farmers. The farmers are attentive and responsive to the FW. Now, the FW explains the purpose of his visit, gives an introduction of his organisation and explains the methods of performing soil testing. The FW asks farmers for any clarifications required. One of the farmers expressed that he did not understand soil testing clearly. The FW nodded his head with a smile and patiently repeated the explanation. While he was trying to show the video on soil testing, his internet connection failed. He promptly takes out his diary and pen and explains the process through drawing. The FW made all possible attempts to explain the concept to the farmers with the available resources.

Scene 2: The farmer appreciates the FWs eagerness to explain soil testing. In the end, the FW asks the farmer about the follow-up meeting and if he can open a WhatsApp group for regular communication and update. The farmers happily accept the request and confirm the next meeting day and time. By then, farmer's children arrive to see their parents and the FW offers them chocolate.

The role play aided in ensuring that the FWs were exposed to communication skills, rapport building methods, and preparation for a technical subject in advance. Role play was designed in such a way that FWs had scope to analyse their own behaviour towards farmer training.

FW's role play analysis

The FWs who were assigned the task of observation were asked to analyse the role play. The observations were made and the corresponding learnings by the FWs were expressed in the pointers below:

- Usually, the FWs never prepared for a session. They just blindly followed the module, which was very monotonous. The FWs learned that it is important to prepare themselves for the training.
- The FWs mentioned that convincing the farmers through videos would be easier, especially for those FWs who do not have much technical knowledge. They also mentioned that it would provide a welcome break from the traditional methods for conveying a message.
- Most of the FWs said that they never considered asking the farmers about their availability for the training and assumed that they could be called anytime. As a result, most of the farmers were absent during the training. FWs were spending too much time on farmer mobilisation and often ended up conducting sessions with just two or three farmers in attendance.
- The FWs agreed that if they reached late for a farmer training session in future, they would apologise to the participants.
- The FWs acknowledged that they did not spend much time with the farmers. By observing the role play they

realized the importance of rapport building which would help them win the trust of the farmers and build a reputation in the community.

- The FWs decided to begin all their sessions by introducing their company, which was essential for the company's branding.
- The FWs realized that they usually failed to ask the farmers about their doubts. They took these sessions as a duty to be conducted in a top-down system. The FWs needed to change their attitude towards the farmer and the way they conducted their sessions.
- In the role play, the FWs tried all the possibilities to convey the message of the training to the farmers using available resources such as paper and pen.
- The FWs appreciated the trainer's strategy of offering chocolates to farmer's children, as it helped them develop a rapport with farmers and their families.

By enacting scenarios like this, the trainees explored how other people were likely to respond to different situations; and trainees got 'a feel' of strategies that were likely to work in a real scenario.

Also, by preparing for a situation using role-play, trainees gained experience and developed self-confidence when it came to handling the situation in real life. The trainees developed quick and instinctively correct responses to situations. This meant that trainees reacted effectively as situations evolved, rather than making mistakes or becoming overwhelmed by events.

The trainees also used role-play to spark brainstorming sessions, to improve communication between team members, and to observe problems or situations from different perspectives.

In the end, the trainer asked the participants to formulate a Job Improvement Plan. This action plan was prepared by each trainee on how they would strategize and reach maximum farmers based on their learnings during the training programme. After the training, the Job Improvement Plan was shared with their seniors.

The seniors further modified the plan in light of their organisational requirements. This was the first time that the FWs were communicating with their programme managers. This was the kind of discussion that was likely to increase the organization's receptivity to new idea/strategies that the employee had acquired through training.

Why Case Study?

After successfully conducting training with FWs, the trainer had another challenge – communicating the importance of online training to employees. During the needs assessment, it was found that the employees were upset and resistant to incorporating the digital method of training. To address this situation, the trainer decided to adopt the Case Study Method. A written case study was given to the trainees (See Box 2).

Box 2

A Company receives an instruction from the head office to digitalize their training. The head office realises that the expense of offline training is excessive and the training impact report has not shown any development. As a result, the management decides to implement online training in each state of India.

The employees belong to a mixed age group of 25-55years. Being familiar with the trainer and classroom setting, the sudden change was not acceptable to some employees.

The employees are anxious that they would lose their jobs if they failed to learn the new online training methods. Some of them consider quitting their jobs after 18 years of service in the company. Some employees were adamant and refused to learn while some others felt that it was the company's new strategy to track employee's learning could result in trust issues between the employees and the employer.

Questions for discussion

Was it possible to implement online training?

Would employees accept online training?

What if an employee is unable to complete the online training course?

Employees were given time to discuss the case study with each other and the discussions held on the following questions and the trainees' responses were noted as follows:

- Is it possible to implement online training?
  - Yes, the expense can be curtailed to a greater extent.
  - Yes, if the employees are given proper training on the training applications.
  - Transparency and honesty between management and employees are essential. The management should talk openly and regularly about what they know and encourage input.
- Would employees accept online training?
  - Yes, the central head should address the employees through video conferencing and share his vision for digitalization. Only then would the employee understand the bigger picture.
  - The cost and impact comparison between offline training and online training would help the employees decide, whether to accept or reject online training.
  - Resistance is usually created because of certain blind spots and attitudes, which the employee have as a result of their preoccupation with the technical aspects of new ideas.
  - The trainees mentioned that the case demonstrated the need for cost reduction. The groups then discussed how existing training methods could be improved and how online

>   training could be made to work effectively. Once they agreed on the new online training method, all employees were to be trained in the new method, and all were to be supervised by senior management.
> - The online training could be both asynchronous or synchronous. This would make learning comfortable and enjoyable.

- If an employee could not complete the online training course?
  - Some employees believed that a target would have to be given and delivery timelines would have to be fixed.
  - The employees would get flexi-time and since the course was online, the employees could complete the subject anywhere and at any time.
  - The employees could be rewarded as they completed a course level. This would motivate the employees to complete the course.
  - Some employees felt that the course completion would have to be linked with the appraisal system.
  - If an employee was taking longer than expected to complete the course, the training manager or department supervisor would have to provide hand-holding support.

The case study method allowed the employees to gain first-hand experience of situations and events. It allowed the trainees to empathize with the protagonist and put him in other people's shoes. The trainees were able to understand managerial dilemmas more compassionately. The case study method facilitated the presentation of the trainee's views and analysis of/to the group.

The case study method, therefore, ensured that the trainees had better interaction and active participation in the session.

In the end, the employees accepted online training. The trainer made a follow-up visit and found trainees were confident with online training. The FCL facilitated processes to ensure robust feedback from employees who shared their challenges and suggestions. This led to improved performance among employees and enhanced productivity. The trainer observed the improvement in the amicability levels in the relationship between the inter and intra FCL teams. The simple fact of knowing that your workforce challenges and suggestions are being listened to is often enough to boost engagement.

Conclusion

It is concluded that role play and case study are effective tools to ensure learning and percolation. The role-play method allowed both an introspective and a retrospective analysis of the situation. The case study presents detailed information about situations and allows trainees to 'feel' the decision maker's position. The application of these methods proves that trainees became sensitive towards the emotions of others along with managing the behaviour, impulses and overall productivity of self. When the workforce feels valued and appreciated and recognized, it delivers measurably enhanced work performance. This leads in the achievement of overall productivity of an organization.

References

Books:

- Kodwani, A. & Raymond, A. (2018). *Employee Training and Development* (7th ed.). Chennai, McGraw Hill Education (India) Private Limited.
- Lynton, R. & Pareek, U. (2011). *Training and Development* (3rd ed.). New Delhi, SAGE Publications India Private Limited.
- Raymond, A.N.(2008). *Employee Training and Development* (4th ed.). India, Mcgraw Hill.

Wg Cdr Rakesh Kumar Prashar

is an internationally certified corporate trainer with over two decades of experience in the Indian Air Force and two decades in the corporate world in the safety domain.

He has a proven track-record as the corporate safety head of various MNCs and Indian corporates in the power sector. As a safety professional he has conducted many audits and investigations for highly reputed corporates in India.

He is the recipient of 'Safety Professional Excellence Award' at the World Environment Summit, 2020 for excellence in safety training as well as 'Best Trainer Award' in 2013. He has conducted over thousand safety training programmes for various corporates in India and abroad as well as soft skills training programmes for various corporates and educational institutions.

He is the author of a book titled 'Organic Safety' and has recently launched his own YouTube channel by the same name. He is currently working on building a meaningful community with a mission of 'Making India Safe'.

He is an empanelled sports commentator with All India Radio and has the unique honour of having covered both World Cup hockey and cricket apart from many other national and international tournaments in hockey and cricket.

6. Train well, stay safe

Making safety training count

By Wg Cdr Rakesh Kumar Prashar

*We don't rise to the level of our expectations,
we fall to the level of our training.*

James Clear

Success in business depends upon the efforts of people working at two different levels - **'Management'** and **'Workers'**. While it is the job of the management to figure out what is to be done so as to 'make maximum profits', it is left to the **'Workers'** to get the job done so as to help 'achieve maximum profits'. It is natural that both have their own expectations. While the management desires an accident free workplace, a productive workforce, lower attrition rates, improved business performance and maximum profits, the workers desire a safe workplace, good health, continued employment, maximum income, and improved career prospects. Even though the expectations of both are actually identical, is it not shocking therefore that nearly 1,000 people lose their lives in workplace related accidents every single day in India.

Why do we hear of such vast number of fatalities in India in the workplace? The answer actually lies in our misplaced faith in 'Luck' and our 'Attitude' of *'Chalta hai'* dominated by the *'Jugaad'* technology, on account of which an accident is always waiting to happen.

As per the **'Accident pyramid theory'** propounded in 1931 by Herbert William Heinrich, 98% of the workplace accidents are attributable to 'Human Factor' while less than 2% accidents fall in the category of 'Unavoidable' accidents. Nearly a century later, this theory still holds good inspite of the tremendous human and technological advancement.

What is indeed shocking is the fact that of these 98% accidents, almost all the people who end up losing their lives in the workplace accidents are the workers who are paid a pittance for the hazardous work that they do. How often have we heard of anyone from the top management losing their lives or getting injured in workplace accidents? Sadly, the workers are blamed for most of the accidents while the management washes its hands off the accidents. Needless to say, while the workers owe it to themselves and their families to work safely, responsibility has been vested in the organisations both statutorily as well as morally, to ensure creation of a safe working environment so that accidents and injuries can be prevented in the workplace.

While it stands to reason that for a company to survive, the business must be profitable, but the same cannot be at the cost of human life. Unfortunately, in an effort to reduce costs in the highly competitive market situation as it exists today, safety generally is the first to take a hit.

Prevention is better than cure

It is common knowledge that it only requires a moment of carelessness on the part of an individual to lead to an accident. Remember the adage, 'savdhani hati, durghatna ghati'. Since almost all workplace fatalities are attributed to 'Human factor', managing human failures is essential to preventing accidents in the workplace. This calls for a pro-active attitude in dealing with workplace hazards which includes continuous enhancement of skills and knowledge through training of all personnel, at all levels.

It is a widely acknowledged fact that 'Accidents don't happen, they are caused'. Well, if accidents are caused, they can be prevented too. Incidentally, all organisations follow the philosophy that 'All accidents are preventable' which is the genesis of their 'Zero Accident, Zero Harm' vision. However, no organisation can ever ensure 100% success in their safety effort just by targeting 'Zero'.

Achieving the goal of 'zero' requires 100% commitment to the cause of safety and even 99.99% will not enable us to achieve the desired results. This clearly means that not one person is to be left out of the ambit whatsoever from the very top to the last man down the line. Training plays a very big role not only in enhancing safety in the workplace, but also in increasing profitability of the organisation. While it is a commonly held view that 'Perfection kills progress', in safety contrary to beliefs, 'Perfection enhances progress'.

Role of training in accident prevention

The root cause for any major problem in the world can be traced back to lack of education. The same holds good in the workplace too. Lack of knowledge not only leads to lack of possibility for personal growth but is also a leading cause of many workplace accidents. Safety training is extremely essential for not only making the employees understand the workplace safety protocols but also create awareness of the organisation's safety vision and goal. They will thus be able to see the 'big picture' and appreciate their role in the overall organisational growth. This will go a long way in helping achieve both the safety as well as business goals of the organisation.

Since the success of our business plans depends entirely on the employees, losing competent employees can have serious repercussions on the business. Preventing accidents at the workplace therefore becomes an overriding priority for every organisation. We may frame the most beautifully written safety policy as well as draft excellent safe operating procedures, but they alone will not ensure an accident free environment. We may also provide the employees the best of the PPE and safety gadgets, but they too will not actually reduce the accidents or the corresponding costs of accidents. Training therefore is extremely critical to workplace safety and plays a very important role in accident prevention.

Safety training helps improve skills and knowledge, develops self-confidence, boosts morale, and improves workplace environment all of which help to improve performance and increased productivity which lead to both organisational as well as personal growth.

Safety training therefore assumes great significance in accident prevention because it encourages wellness of both the personnel as well as the organisation.

Drawbacks in the current safety training system

I have had the opportunity of conducting hundreds of safety audits and accident investigations and over a thousand safety training sessions in various corporates at all levels from the top management to the grass root level workers. I would like to share a few shocking facts that I have observed during these:

- *'Productivity will be hampered'*, is the general excuse of the managers for not sparing employees for safety training sessions. However, when this statement fails to elicit the required response, the next salvo that is fired is *'My staff is trained and experienced'*. Not detailing employees for safety training is a serious management issue as productivity cannot take precedence over saving lives.

- *'Safety training sessions are boring'*, is the general refrain of the employees who are not willing to attend safety training sessions because they are in fact neither interesting nor engaging. This not only raises questions about the quality of the training, but also the trainers.

- It is common to see standard training modules being used in the corporates year on year. This not only raises questions on the effectiveness, but the very rationale of the training itself.

- Training is carried out with the purpose of ensuring paperwork and not with the intention of genuine skill development and knowledge building that it is meant to be.

- Almost all personnel in the top management have neither attended any full day safety training nor are they interested in doing so citing 'lack of time' as the main excuse.

- Most employees at the middle levels too have neither attended any full day safety training nor wish to do so too. If the people who are expected to oversee hazardous working are not exposed to continual safety training, how can they be expected to deliver results that are expected of them consistently?

- Many employees in the lower levels who are directly exposed to the hazards, have not even gone through the formality of a formal safety induction. As such, many workers, though exceedingly good in their job, are not even aware of some of the basic health and safety rules.

The situation is really frightening. If we really want to save human lives, this situation has to change, and the management has a very big role to play in this. By ensuring regular and continual safety training of the employees, the management will not only make the workplace environment safe and healthy, but also make the workplace a happy place to work. This will help improve morale of the employees thus increasing performance and improving productivity also.

Making safety training relevant

In order to ensure that safety programmes succeed as envisaged, all employees need to be motivated and committed. Safety training is the best investment that an organisation can ever make, but only if it is made relevant? But how can we make safety training relevant.

A few steps that can help make safety training meaningful, purposeful, and also effective, include:

- Make safety training sessions interesting and engaging. Do not fall in the rut of only using speech or PowerPoint presentations for safety sessions. Try using videos, quiz, and games in your training sessions to present information in a different manner to make the sessions more interesting and relevant. This will not only keep the audience engaged, but also ensure 'active participation'.

- Ensure that the top management also attends safety training sessions regularly. This not only sends a message that **'we care'** but that safety is important across all levels of the organisation. By not attending safety sessions, the top management sends extremely negative signals to the employees.

- Ensure that personnel right down to the grass root level workers whether full-time or even part-time are detailed and also must undergo safety training as appropriate.

- Ensuring that all new employees are briefed properly and appropriately, not only makes them aware of the safety rules and procedures, but also impresses upon them the need to ensure safety in the workplace.

- Training to be successful must be dynamic as it loses its significance if it does not keep pace with the technological advancements in the workplace.

- While it is essential to cover all workplace specific safety practices including accident statistics, common types of injuries etc. do not hesitate to step out of the routine. Safety training to be successful, must be holistic and all-encompassing without sacrificing relevancy. Remember, safety is not a '9–5 Job', but a '24x7 Value'.

- Do not use training rooms only for conducting training sessions. Focus on conducting training sessions 'on the ground' as well as in the labour camps where the workers are most receptive.

- Training is not a one session act, but a continuous process. Since the average memory span of the people is generally short, it is advisable to conduct continual safety training sessions once every quarter for it to be really effective. If the training is followed up with monitoring employees behaviour on the ground or in the workplace, it will make the training stick, making it even more effective.

- Take feedback and constantly evaluate your training to achieve continuous improvement.

- Do not hesitate to seek the help of specialist trainers who are really passionate about safety. This is actually recommended as the preferred option. Remember the adage '*Ghar ki murgi, daal barabar*'.

- Last but not the least, focus on changing the 'Attitude' and Behaviour' of the participants as it will have a long-lasting effect on the safety performance in the organisation. These training sessions must be conducted at least once a quarter to be genuinely effective. We will do well to remember that '***Behaviour drives people, but people drive business***'.

You must make all out efforts to ensure that your participants walk out of the session happy. Remember an employee who walks out happy after a safety training session is a 'lead magnet' for future safety training sessions and an advocate for safety. Business legend Richard Branson explained it so beautifully when he said, *"Train people so well that they can leave anytime, but treat them so well that they don't want to leave ever"*.

Do not wait for something unfortunate to happen, to plan for training, instead train and motivate your team so well that such a situation never arises.

Advantages of safety training

Conducting regular safety training is vital to building a safe, healthy, and productive work environment in the organisation as it will ultimately benefit the company and its reputation. Some of the advantages associated with safety training include:

- It helps promote awareness of the workplace hazards which enables workers to take precautionary measures and the supervisors to ensure the same.
- It helps reduce accidents and injuries as workers are educated routinely on safe working procedures.
- It helps avoid financial loss likely to be incurred on account of accidents.
- It helps improve morale and establish loyalty as inspired workers are proud to be part of the company.

- It helps avoid the stress that accidents and ill health cause.
- It helps encourage and emphasise the need for proper use, care and maintenance of PPE as required.
- It helps in better implementation of safety protocols.
- It helps workers to operate sophisticated and advanced equipment employed in the workplace effectively.
- It helps enhance the quality because a safe working environment is an efficient environment.
- It helps ensure timely and safe completion of tasks which also translates into increased productivity and more profits.
- It helps updating everyone about the changes in systems, procedures and protocols affecting workplace safety.
- It helps meet the statutory requirements of protecting the health and safety of employees.
- It helps establish employee engagement in safety.
- It helps develop a positive safety culture in the organisation, where working safely comes naturally to everyone.

Since prevention of accidents has a direct and positive impact on the company, expenditures in terms of trainer costs as also the participants loss of productivity for the day should be seen as an 'Investment' and not a 'Cost'.

The need for changing our attitude towards safety training

Keeping a positive mindset even in a negative environment is extremely important and this can not only lead to a welcome change but can even result in tremendous success. Those who only look at the present and resist change by refusing to step out of their comfort zones, only create sorrow for themselves.

If we wish to succeed and stay relevant in the future, we must continuously evolve. It may be challenging initially, but it will be exciting and rewarding in the long run.

While we all agree that we desire a safe workplace, we must remember that a safe workplace cannot be achieved by 'desiring' alone, but by 'striving' together. If safety is integrated into our lives and our business, we will not only see *safety work for us*', but will also see '*safer, motivated, and more compliant employees work for us*'. This will enable us to have a positive safety-oriented culture in our organisation as well as a progressive, more positive, and safe business.

While workplace safety is a profoundly serious business, safety training is a '**Low-cost**' but '**High impact**' way of not only saving lives, but also businesses. Post Covid-19, the training scenario has changed dramatically especially in India, and we have seen a distinctive rise in e-learning as well as digital platforms. Research also suggests that online training might be here to stay. With almost every person carrying a smart phone these days, training is within easy reach of all and as such safety training too can reach the millions of workers who are not only our frontline warriors but the agents of making our dreams come true.

Can we forget that our workplace is our 'karam-bhoomi' (place of action) where we aim to achieve our business goals without spilling even a drop of blood, and not a 'ran-bhoomi' (battleground) where our success is laid on the amount of the blood that is shed. Our karam-bhoomi not only provides us with our salary which is the most important consideration when choosing a job, but also affords us the freedom to live our life and design the life of our family. If any untoward incident occurs there, we will be failing collectively in our duties to keep our 'karam-bhoomi' safe and healthy.

We therefore need to look at safety training not from where we are 'perched', but from a different 'perspective' so that we can see the 'bigger picture'. Only then can we work towards working for the betterment of our workforce as well as our business and fulfilment of our dream of **'*Making India Safe*'**.

Ruchi Chauhan

Ruchi Chauhan is a development professional with over 12 years in the fields of logistics and research. She has an established record of providing value to entities in the corporate as well as social sectors across the globe.

Ruchi's professional practice has been enriched by her incorporation of psychology for monitoring, evaluation, project management, and strategy building in domains like education, life skill coaching, gender equality, and public health. Her mission is to connect corporates to NGOs for making meaningful communities possible.

Ruchi is a Buddhist who thinks, speaks, and acts out her conviction that if one makes consistent efforts in any direction without seeking any praise or approval one can not only make a great difference in the lives of other people but in one's own life.

7. 5 hacks for work-life balance

Understanding how pausing, eliminating, connecting, practicing, and surrendering can help you get your cake and eat it too

By Ruchi Chauhan

No one on his deathbed ever said,
'I wish I had spent more time at the office'.

Paul Tsongas, Politician

Life is an incredible journey where every moment is both a treasure hunt and a battle. In between seeking our treasures and fighting it out, striking balance between life and work is of utmost importance. You have to be something of a Ninja to walk this tightrope between home and office. You not only risk falling off the rope but also dying a slow death in your never-ending effort to keep on the rope!

Life has become fast post-liberalization. The globe has shrunk. Countries in the West have used the access to new markets like India after liberalization to optimise their supply chains. They have recalibrated their businesses in a manner that gives them effortless access to raw material and labour from countries like India at price that are cheaper than back home. However, when one looks at the impact it has had in India, life in the workplace, at home and in the social sphere has become chaotic thanks to the long hours, demanding KRAs and never-ending waves of deadlines. One is naturally expected in this scenario to compromise on the family and social front and to master the art of juggling in both the personal and professional fronts.

It is as if we are not human beings but trained robots who will only pause work to consume food, water, and air. If the system had its way, we would only be allowed free time to reboot for upcoming deadlines, and presentations, and leave us to figure out how to attend the needs of everyone in the family. Visits to aunts, and attending weddings and baby-showers would have to wait.

As if these pulls and pressures were not enough, we now have Corona! One wonders what additional burdens will be added to our lives in the post-lockdown world. Jobs cuts are already adding fuel to the fire.

Like Iron Man, digitization did come to rescue for workers of all kinds but unfortunately conditions apply there as well. We are expected to operate from homes without defined work-hours. Work is just floating all over the place, particularly in India, where work from home is an alien concept in most of corporate setups.

Not everyone has home spaces big enough to accommodate work from home. Then there are many who do not have the necessary hardware. Micro-managing, digitization of all aspects of a day's work ranging from discussions to presentations, and reporting, takes time and effort. To these chores, there is added household work that has to be dealt with in absence of domestic help, and the responsibility of keeping kids engaged in constructive activities. There is the challenge of channelizing their energies and manage their increased screen time as well. All these factors contribute to the usual stress and anxiety of individuals.

Situations like the current crisis impact all eight dimensions of wellness identified by the Substance Abuse and Mental Health Services Administration (SAMHSA): Physical, intellectual, emotional, social, spiritual, vocational, financial, and environmental. It is important to point out here that neither homemakers nor professionals are immune to the impact of a crisis of this magnitude.

Neera Chabra, a senior healthcare professional said, "The increased screen time, digital meetings, webinars and the absence of a domestic help is overwhelming. Initially, it was alright. Now both my husband and I find it very suffocating to function as working professionals. I am honestly unable to decide if I should work, clean or cook!"

A survey conducted by The India@Work on 585 Gen-Y, Senior-level professionals, across industries, was published in the Economic Times in January 2020. The report revealed that around 90 percent of professionals aspire to shift towards a more flexible working environment. This further boosts their productivity.

The survey also suggested that longer the commuting time is inversely related to time spent with the family and on ensuring physical, psychological and spiritual well-being.

Shailendra, an IT Professional, is of the opinion that WLB is a fad. "I don't think anything can be done about it. We cannot separate our work from our personal lives. The offshore clients and deliverables are pretty taxing. The fear of losing one's job is an ever-present reality. If you complain, you are quickly reminded by the management how lucky you are to have a job and the added flexibility of working from home. They say if you still cry, then there is no end to it, they tell you."

This brings me to the story of Raj who is newly married and has created a new home with his wife in the city. As a consultant, Raj is always on the edge with his tight deadlines, and multiple projects. He travels routinely, and also has the responsibility of retired parents and two younger siblings living in Pilibhit, Uttar Pradesh. He feels that work-life balance is a distant dream. "To maintain a good standard of living and provide for two household setups, I have to slog myself. I cannot dream of pursuing the mirage of work-life balance, which is nothing beyond jargon. Home and family can be managed; our loved ones have to understand that we are doing this for them. Who else I am doing all this for? I know work, health, and family are equally important but what can I do? How will I pay my bills if I don't work?" he said.

Of course, Raj has his reasons for saying what he is but it is actually possible to achieve work-life balance? I have been researching on this subject for some time and have read hundreds of webpages so far.

I am happy to share that I have personally met and spoken to dozens of people who have achieved work-life balance, or have a positive perspective on it. Their guidance is helping me steer my own life in that direction. So, here is my summary of life-work hacks I have picked on the way that I believe can help anyone who seeks a more balanced life.

Hack one: Reason your reason

As long as we live, personal and professional life will always involve stretching and constant fine-tuning, which can prove to be taxing. Nowadays, individuals seek extrinsic pleasures, instead of intrinsic growth. They lose their grip on their inner life for tangible gains in the world.

Caught in the small stuff, we step on a treadmill that we are unable to get off all our lives. PAUSE to stop what we are doing and taking a Positive Action Utilising Systematic Energy around us through these hacks is the very first step in the direction of change. With time, accountabilities both at a professional, and personal front increase, and then the survival becomes the number one priority. Balance is the last thing that comes to the mind in such situation. I would say merely pausing and examining one's life without judgment is in itself a transformative experience. Stop getting breathless, and do as little as possible and use the time to consider how you have been leading your life, and handling areas like work, relationships, family, friendships, and social responsibilities.

Press the pause button.

Hack two: Stop squeezing the ras out of the gulla

After you have pressed the pause button, identify areas where you have been squeezing the fun out. Consider what you have been doing at the cost of ignoring daily exercise, good sleep, and healthy eating. What if making random food choices, and being glued to the computer for long hours giving you. Is the compensation for the damage you are doing to yourself in these area worth the loss in the key areas of your well-being?

Do a cost-benefit analysis and stop carrying the world on your shoulders.

What is life without fun?

Cut the activities that are squeezing the fun out of your life and keep them to the rare minimum.

Piyali Sharma, a psychologist, says, "It is often an array of excuses that professionals give to themselves in the name of work to avoid dealing with other key areas in their lives. Since none of the other things that matter bring financial gain, they feel those aspects can be skipped. One certainly has to earn a living and maintain a standard of life, but at what cost? What will you do when despite earning a bomb you do not have health, friends, and family to enjoy? One needs to make a conscious choice and strike towards balance."

Here is how you make a beginning in the direction of disengaging from the inessential:

- Take **conscious small breaks** from the digital screen, meetings
- **Move away from your station** between breaks for mobility,
- **Keep drinking water and eat healthy** food such as fruits, and nuts at infrequent intervals.
- **Walk or do stretching exercises** for about 20 or 30 minutes if cannot do so for an hour
- **Sleep for 6-7 hours.** Set up a routine so you sleep and wake up at the same time every day,
- Take a **digital detox** 35 mins before you sleep

These are very basic steps. However, it is not enough to commit them to memory. You need to act on them. Unless implemented, they won't bring your life-work balance. As Richie Norton puts it 'Intellect without implementation is ignorance, not intelligence.'

The process of implementation and change requires complete ownership and responsibility from the seeker! The shift from reason to action is a sign of growth and a step forward towards the goal.

Hack three: Connect with the inner symphony or infinite space

Every human being is governed by the eight dimensions of wellness – physical, intellectual, emotional, social, spiritual, vocational, financial, and environmental.

These are interdependent.

I was in school when a yogi told me, "One must always aspire for spiritual growth as it leads to socio-psychological and intellectual growth as well."

In my practice of Nichiren Buddhism, I learned that change is the only powerful and constant process. The appreciation and gratitude towards one's own self and others have the power to change one's core beliefs. When one takes complete responsibility for one's word, thought and deed as a mission, one is able to change one's karma and improve life on a daily basis through the chanting of the mantra 'Nam Myoho Renge Kyo'.

The sangha I am part of is led by oriental philosopher Dr. Daisaku Ikeda, who has inspired millions like me across the world.

Thanks to this transformative practice, I have become a self-accepting individual. I have also become self-forgiving. I work towards resolving an issue instead of blaming myself for it as I would earlier.

Everyone needs a spiritual anchor sooner or later in life. One's choice of path is a personal matter. You could choose your own path like I did. Connect to a sangha, or meditate yourself, de-stress and connect with the inner self. Stay motivated and joyful as you address the challenges thrown at you by life.

Hack four: Keep balancing as this is a journey not a destination

Do not expect overnight results. Rome, it is known, was not built in a day! Also, even after you reach a point where you feel you have attained balance, there will be forces that will disturb the equilibrium and force you to recalibrate your response.

Make sure that the targets you set for yourself are realistic. Deeply rooted patterns take time to erase. Stay committed and take keep taking tiny consistent actions and ensure that the momentum is kept!

Says Wayne Dyner, "Getting in balance is not so much about adopting new strategies to change your behavior, as it is about realigning yourself in all your thoughts to create a balance between what you desire and how you conduct your life daily."

I share these hacks with confidence because once upon a time, I too was a victim of work-life imbalance, spent a lot of my time giving excuses to self but nothing helped till I began taking conscious steps in the direction.

Hack five: Enter the state of surrender to Sri Sri Bob Marley

Be a pioneer. A pioneer is one who leads by his actions. Bob Marley used his music to generate momentum to spread the message of 'Rastafari' in the 1930s in support of the Jamaican Nationalist Marcus Garvey who urged African-Americans to be proud of their race and return to Africa their ancestral homeland.

Both his music as well as the concept of 'Rastafari' was well accepted across the globe, and is revered till date. His work transcends time and space, as the foundation of his music is the human condition, which is a constant condition amid the job cuts, widening income gaps, and discrimination based on gender, caste or creed, and terrorism, etc.

The ego makes big plans and enjoys struggle and pain. However, the light in us only shines when we pause as suggested in hack 1 and surrender to something higher than us. In this state of surrender, miracles happen. It is not the person we are surrendering to who is performing the miracle but our own Buddha nature shining forth. It is therefore important to surrender to someone you are not ashamed of surrendering to, someone who can show you the mirror of reality.

Finally, embracing change and self-improvisation are your two key weapons on the path. Luckily, the ability to exercise these two weapons lies with you. One need not to look outside for effecting a transformation. Just stay connected with the anchor within. Change will follow.

These five hacks for attaining work-life balance have worked miracles in my life, and they have changed the lives of people I shared them with. Now, dear reader, the ball is in your court.

Are you ready for a more confident, calmer, and happier version of you?

Are you ready to rise and shine?

Subodh Langde

is a textile engineer and management graduate with over 27 years in the textile and IT Industries.

He recently found his life's calling as a Parenting Coach & Student Success Coach.

His professional interests span the fields of education, career guidance, and the corporate world. In his practice, he works with parents as well as the youth by using the scientific methodology 'P-F-S', which emphasises Plan, Focus, and Succeed.

Subodh was born, raised, and married in Mumbai, which is where he lives with his wife and two children.

8. It takes a village

By Subodh Langde

There are two gifts we can give our children.
One is roots, and the other is wings.

Anonymous

When the theme of this book *Rise and Shine* was agreed upon by my fellow-writers, I had no clue what I would write on. My mind went into flashback mode looking for topics that would do justice to the theme and I finally decided that I would write about my life journey, which is a story of how I 'rose' in life and 'shone' with the passage of time. It would also be about the lessons I learned along the way.

I had a long-standing desire to be an author. This book was therefore a good place to start. Reading has always been an inspiring experience for me. All these years of reading have seeded in me the desire to write. I feel that I have a lot to share with the world. There were however some limiting beliefs that had held me back so far. I wondered who would be interested in reading my story. I also had doubts surrounding my knowledge of English. Was it polished enough? I had been made to feel inadequate by my poor grasp of grammar in the past. I also thought that my vocabulary was way too poor, and I had no knowledge of publishing, which would supposedly call for a huge investment on my part. Today, as a part of the TTOT tribe, my dream of becoming an author is finally coming true.

A Parenting Coach is born-

So, what follows is the story of how my life journey from my humble beginnings to a position that made me a global citizen created in me this intense desire to serve the needs of children as well as. It is a life story that climaxes with my birth as a Parenting Coach.

On a breezy morning in Milan last year, I was staring out of the window of my hotel as I sipped hot black coffee at the river outside with its sailing boats, smiling faces of children, and tourists having fun. My mind raced back to my children, their childhood, and my extended family. I began reflecting on all the past events that had combined to bring me where I was. Suddenly, without warning, tears began rolling down my eyes. Feeling proud, standing there at Milan, I was happy and content. And then, in the very next moment, I was sad about being away from my family.

I was on an exciting project that would keep me away from home for six months.

As I thought about the two conflicting emotions I was experiencing, I began to focus on my inner voice, which became louder with every minute. The truth was that despite the scenic surroundings and beautiful weather and an assignment that anybody in my position would die for, my heart missed my family. It was something way more precious than anything money could buy. The presence of my children and my extended family – my people - around me, at that moment, was what mattered to me the most.

My son Sarthak, was already a computer engineer. He is currently pursuing his master's degree in Artificial Intelligence from a leading institute in Germany. Janhvi, my daughter, a graduate in Mass Media, is preparing for her civil service exam. She turned author with the publication of her book *Money Masters for Kids.*

My wife was a trainer and counsellor. She was working then in a school as a teacher's trainer for the ECCEd course.

My father, my family, and my friends all were in good health. Everything was going great. I had everything any man could ask for.

I had no reason to complain.

Yet, on that day, I asked myself if what I was doing in my life was all I wanted to do?

I washed the mug and kept it aside. Though I was hungry, I ignored the cravings. I lay down on the red sofa in my room, and closed my eyes. My life began to flash before my eyes like a film.

I was born in Vikhroli, Mumbai, and brought up in a typical middle-class family. I was the eldest of three siblings, and also the most mischievous. My father was a very strict and disciplined man. He was a government employee. My mother was a homemaker. She was a very loving and caring person. Though we were just us five members in the family, like five fingers in a hand, we were held together like a closed fist. My mother's warmth, and my father's commitment to our near and dear ones gave us the wonderful gift of a huge joint family. Our relatives were always around, and there was always someone around to talk to and play with.

My childhood brimmed over with playful fun and mischief. I played all kinds of sports. I played cards and was a champ on the carom board. We also had a long list of outdoor games that kids today don't play like kite-flying, playing with marbles, laghori, viti-dandu, dabba express, langdi, chipri, aatya-patya, football, cycling, swimming and cricket.

My cricket memories are special. I broken the window panes of nearly all the buildings in my lane. Cricket remains my favourite sport. Despite spending long hours playing, education was accorded the highest priority in our family. As my father encountered some medical challenges, the family's care became my responsibility as an elder son, early in my life. I chose to go for a diploma (3 years) in engineering rather than doing 10+2 and then degree (4 years) so I could land a job faster.

I took admission in Sasmira, which is one of the best textile engineering colleges in India. I cleared my diploma with first class, and was in the top 3 in my batch.

I joined government-owned National Textile Corporation as an apprentice in June 1990. At 21, I was one of the youngest employee at the NTC's Poddar Processors unit. This was my first job and my first experience of working in an organization. The huge setup, the sprawling mill property with its various departments, big machines, massive boilers, and the sound of mill sirens were all overwhelming for me. The most touching moment of all was the day I received my first salary, which was given to me in the form of cash in an envelope unlike today, when one's salary is either deposited directly in the bank account or handed over in the form of a cheque.

I was learning fast and growing in the organization. My seniors were guiding and advising me whenever required. They would share their experiences and life learning with me and school me in the dos and the don'ts. After I had worked for a few years in the textile industry, the intense environment and working conditions began to enervate me a little. This put me in thinking mode. I began to wonder if it was time to explore a life beyond the textile industry.

I cleared my HSC exam as an external student, which allowed me to study on my own during my night shifts. Daytime was for rest and playing cricket.

I kept at it till I earned my bachelor's degree in Sociology through distance education.

Around this time, the textile industry began to die. Many units were declared sick. A few were closed down by the government, and there were hints and whispers that big changes were in store for our mill as well. 'What next?' was an important question that could no longer be ignored. I was already married, and we had a son too. I had seen enough at work to know that in every organisation, the management plays an important role, which made me to attempt an entrance test for a management course.

Before I took the plunger, I discussed the idea with both my families, my parents as well as in-laws. They were all very supportive. They understood and accepted my decision to quit my job.

After having worked for seven years, I had the distinction of being the youngest employee in NTC to opt for voluntary retirement. The money I received from NTC helped me to fund my higher studies with ease. I had also saved some money in the last few years. The combined kitty kept the household fires burning for two years that I invested in earning a management degree. My family supported me mentally and financially during this crucial phase of life.

It was an amazing experience to be back in college after seven years. Sitting on a classroom bench and studying was a different experience now that I had worked for seven years in the textile industry.

It was a little difficult to concentrate on studies. Adapting to the new schedule, sitting with youngsters, and experiencing new learning methodologies like case studies, role play, submissions, and projects did not come easily to me.

After I earned my Masters in Management Studies degree with first class, it was time to go 'dream job hunting'. I had specialized in Systems Management. It was the very first batch with the specialisation at Mumbai University. With seven years of experience in the manufacturing industry, my professor suggested that I explore IT as a career segment.

Unfortunately, it was not that easy. The dot.com bubble had just burst, Y2K had impacted much of the IT industry, and it was therefore a struggle to land a job in the IT sector. I was unemployed for six months.

My first break was with CMC, and later with CMS, Hutchison Max Telecom (It was later christened Orange and is now known as Vodafone), and Clover Technologies. This was when life changed for me, and all the hard work began to pay.

In 2004, I joined Capgemini, which was close to my house. I had to report on European timings, which brought me a bonus that was far precious than any joy money could bring me. I could now dedicatedly pay attention to my children.

I could devote quality time to family thanks also to the fact that I was working five-days-a-week. Saturdays and Sundays were holidays.

I helped my children with their studies. I taught them the importance of values and culture. Basic concepts were imparted in a fun manner, which made them learn faster and better. Languages were taken care of by my wife, Rashmi. She made a point to explain everything to them in three languages - English, Marathi (my mother tongue), and Gujarati (her mother tongue).

This trilingual media was observed diligently irrespective of the subject.

We had lots of fun. Those were the golden days of our lives. The children got love, care, and warmth of the family from both sides of the family. Here Aajji-Aajoba, Aatya-Mama, Chachu-Chachi; and there, Dadi-Dada, Nani-Nana, Masis, and Mamas. Both me and my wife are eldest among our respective set of siblings, which has made us extremely adaptable and flexible in our approach to raising our children. It was also our good fortune to have grown up in big joint families. Our children have had the advantage of being in constant exposure to different cultures, traditions, values, and varieties of food thanks to the diversity of family members surrounding us. This diversity and extended family atmosphere has contributed toward making children successful in their curricular as well as extra-curricular efforts.

In 2008, we shifted to Bhandup and our children moved from the State Board to ICSE Board. We collectively took a decision to not have a TV in our new house. This helped us spend quality time with each other through the day and especially during meals. Reading became our favourite pastime. Together, we read newspapers and fiction as well as non-fiction books, and slowly, a library began to take shape in our home.

The books improved the kids' vocabulary, corrected their grammar and taught them to articulate their point of view confidently. It also helped them with their academics.

Of course, we bought a computer as their education demanded it. We watched movies and shows with them when we wished to. However, we were particular about what we watched. I would choose movies in Hindi, Marathi, English, Gujarati, Tamil or Telugu. We would occasionally go out for watching movies followed by meals at restaurants with our families or families of our friends.

At our new home, the next-door neighbour and soon the entire floor became our extended family. After shifting from Vikhroli, every Sunday, it became a ritual to visit our old home to be with the extended family. It gave us the feeling of completeness. And on all the birthdays and anniversaries, we would congregate without fail. My parents kept us bonded. My mother would complain if we failed to call or missed a Sunday.

At night before sleeping, I used to play different games with children, and ask them different questions, riddles, and puzzles. I did not want my children to only focus on studies. My daughter Janhvi has always loved books and reading, and Sarthak, my son, favoured gadgets. I was happy with their choices but wanted them to have the right attitude while doing anything irrespective of the outcome. And my wife Rashmi used to tell them that being a good human is more important than anything you do. It is, in fact, more important than the profession you choose.

On the job front, I kept getting on-site opportunities and work-related assignments all over Europe. I had the opportunity to visit London, Paris, Grenoble, Lyon, and Milan. It was in Milan that evening that I received a call from my cousin that got me thinking. She was worried about her the casual attitude of her children towards academics. As a parent, I understood her concerns about the kids for their future. This was when I first began my preliminary research into the subject of parenting. In September 2019, after I returned to India, I continued with my day job but my heart and soul were given to researching parenting.

I began noticing the different parenting styles being followed in the society I was part of, and also how they were impacting the children.

It dawned upon me that it was time for some major changes in my life. This was an area where I could help and be of service to so many people. My wife and I have always been extremely family-focused, and have also loved being around people. We have enjoyed the lasting trust of our neighbours as well as our friends. Some considered us role models and sought our guidance on issues related to the family, kids, studies, careers, and parenting discipline. We were influential in our extended social circle and had a positive impact on the families associated with us either by blood or social ties.

Finally, after much deliberation, my wife and I decided that we would henceforth help families dealing with challenges pertaining to raising children. We would contribute our mite to help raising healthy, happy and constructive individuals capable of deep, nourishing and stable relationships. So, that, dear friends is how after having spent 27 years in a corporate job, I decided to follow my inner calling to work with human beings.

I was done working with computers and machines.

My mission is to help families achieve their parenting goals while honouring the uniqueness of the child. I am sure you will agree that what a parent, any parent, wants is to secure the well-being and safety of his or her children, and equip them to deal with life as moral and productive adults connected to their traditions. I realized as I researched the subject that worldwide, more than three crore babies are added to the world through unplanned pregnancies. Our society trains people for different kinds of jobs and skills like programming, hairdressing, law, teaching, and medicine but there is no training that prepares parents for parenting. We just tend to copy what we have observed in our families or our society.

Much of that wisdom is still relevant but it is criminal to ignore the many other resources on parenting that we have at our disposal today. We need not do things just because that is the way they have always been done.

When I resigned from my job on 14th January 2020, I had the opportunity to work with my wife Rashmi for the first time. We have made giant strides in the last few months and have realised that there is an urgent need to build a community of like-minded people who trust each other and are willing to discuss every conceivable aspect of the collective responsibility of raising good human beings. It is not for nothing that people have said that it takes a village to raise a child. It is imperative that such a rich, enlightened and diverse village be created through our collective effort with the singular aim of creating kinder, happier, and more compassionate citizens of the world.

Be the village our children deserve.

Cdr K Vijay Kumar

has spent over two decades in the Indian Navy from 1975 to 1998 where he was involved in training of Naval personnel and in operational roles as Meteorological and Oceanographic forecaster. He was a member of the 10th Indian oceanographic expedition to Antarctica in 1990-91. He has participated in several oceanographic cruises on Indian oceanographic research ships of the National Institute of Oceanography, and has also been part of a research cruise in the Indian Ocean with a Soviet oceanographic research vessel.

After retirement from the Indian Navy, he has trained over ten thousand entry and middle-level managers from multinational corporations in areas of Managerial skills, Personal Effectiveness, Leadership, Communication, and Emotional Intelligence.

Cdr K Vijay Kumar has a Master's degree in Mathematics, Diplomas in Management, and a Master's degree in Yogic Sciences from Mangalore University, which he acquired at the age of 66 years. He has been an avid practitioner of Yoga for the past 30 years, and is a passionate advocate for using yogic principles to mold character.

9. Yoga for character building

By Cdr K Vijay Kumar

We are what our thoughts have made us; so, take care about what you think. Words are secondary. Thoughts live; they travel far.

Swami Vivekananda

A society is known by the character of its people. When the character of the people comprising a particular society is good, crime rates are low. People help each other. The society is happy and peaceful. Good character is therefore the very foundation of any society. A society comprising individuals without character either descends into a quagmire of crime or turns into a place of apathy where selfishness rules the roost and no one cares for others.

Proper parenting and an educational system that can imbibe good character traits is essential for progress of any society or nation. In this article, I am going to argue that Patanjali Yoga Sutras compiled by Maharshi Patanjali 2500 years ago can be a good training manual for building good character in youngsters.

Character is a set of acceptable behaviours in any healthy society. It is a set of good habits that are formed when one repeats certain behaviours over a time. Habits are born of thoughts. Having noble thoughts therefore ensures good behaviour and good habits, and shape good characters.

The Patanjali Yoga Sutra, compiled by Maharshi Patanjali 2500 years ago has for its subject the management of thoughts. We can therefore use the concepts of the Yoga sutras to modify our thoughts and character.

Character is a hidden thing in a person. Like the roots of a tree, it remains hidden from the causal eye. However, it is arguably the most important part of a tree and central to its survival.

A plant may look healthy from outside, but if the roots are rotten, the tree will soon die. It is possible for the personality or the external manifestation of a person to be good or even attractive, while his or her character is compromised inside. Such a person cannot survive in the long run. Discrepancies or lack of alignment between outer persona and inner characters are common experience. Often, when a company recruits an employee based on outer personality, we may discover very soon that the value system of the new hire does not match with that of the company. It is likely that such an employee may lose his job because his values and those of the company are at odds. It is therefore important that we possess the character that makes us deserving of all good things. Deception can give us temporary gains but, in the end, it is character that really matters.

Good thoughts result in good actions, good actions become good habits and a set of good habits result in good character. Good character results in good destiny.

Truthfulness–

I once had recruited an employee and found him to be sincere and effective in the very first month with me. Unfortunately for him, the verification process of his resume threw up the fact that he had lied in the resume to cover up a gap in his appointment. If he had told the truth about the gap, it would have been acceptable. But a lie was not. We had to part with him.

Honesty–

In a company where I worked, we had to train and test fresh hires for three months before they were assigned to projects. The company allowed a maximum of three attempts in each of papers, failing which a candidate was expected to resign. To help their junior colleagues who were yet to take the tests, three trainee employees took screenshots of the online questions and leaked them to others. This was discovered. The ones who leaked the information were dismissed due to this well-meaning but dishonest practice.

Emotional self-control-

A former colleague had parked his car in a no-parking area in the city. On returning, he saw a policeman locking the car tyres with a chain. Suddenly, his emotions went out of control, he started the car and drove through the policeman who had stood in front of him to stop the car. The policeman had to save himself by hanging onto the wiper blades for over 1 km the man drove madly. He was eventually stopped, arrested and tried and got three years in jail for culpable homicide.

Forgiveness-

Sometimes, we may not burst in anger but harbour a simmering resentment towards someone who may have hurt us. Such resentment is like a slow fire silently burning us from the inside. The way out is to douse this fire with the waters of forgiveness. It is better to forgive and just be alert so that we are learn our lesson and do not get cheated again.

Empathy-

Empathy is a character trait that helps us understand the emotions of others and facilitates the feeling of on our part of what the other person is feeling. It is like putting ourselves in the other person's shoes. Only then do we know where the shoe hurts.

I remember the case of a colleague who was murdered by her husband at home. This was a case of a bad marriage. I discovered from others that she had always worn a sad and hassled look. If only her manager had made an empathic statement like 'You look sad', she would probably have opened up and some professional counselling is all it would have taken for the couple to get out of what was clearly a bad marriage.

Having a purpose in life-

We must contemplate why we have come into this world. If we do not find meaning in whatever we are doing, life becomes dull. We may have riches but it is not possible to enjoy those riches without having a sense of meaning and accomplishment.

It is imperative that every individual contemplate the purpose of his or her life, his or her reason for being here. Once the purpose is understood, we can derive our mission statement, which states what our contributions to the world would be. It is the purpose and the mission statement that helps one set goals that create a meaningful and purposeful life.

Responsibility-

What do parents do when their little children accidentally bang their heads against a wall? Parents bang the wall 'to punish it' and blame it for causing them hurt. The children immediately calm down and readily believe that it is the wall, which is to be blamed and that the kid is not at fault at all. The problem is that we continue this attitude of blaming others whenever things go wrong even after we reach adulthood and enter the workplace. Blaming others when we should be owning up to our faults and undertaking course correction becomes a deadly habit that retards our growth.

Attitude –

To succeed in the world, we need knowledge, skill, and attitude. Knowledge and skill are not enough for success. The right attitude is a must for using the knowledge and skills we have acquired. Attitude is like the hidden part of an iceberg which keeps it stable. Knowledge and skill are the visible parts.

Discipline-

Discipline is important in all phases of our life. Can we behave in an undisciplined manner on roads choked with traffic? If we do not take the correct lanes or do not stop at traffic signals, we are likely to cause traffic jams, or worse, meet with accidents. In life, progress only comes to us if we adhere to self-discipline and ensure that we keep our promises, and be on time.

Motivation-

We cannot remain effective for long if we are demotivated. We cannot hope that others will motivate us. We must stay motivated even when things do not go our way. Optimism helps in such difficult times. Optimists do not lose their self-esteem.

They attempt what they have fallen short of once again with a renewed vigour. We must all rise and shine.

Trust–

We all have a need to be trusted because no task, however small, can be accomplished without others trusting us and cooperating with us. We must earn that trust by displaying certain behaviours. Being kind and respectful, not just externally, but from the heart is important. We must genuinely wish other people well without judging their status. We must carry no grudges and forgive others who may have antagonized us. Keeping promises, being accountable and knowing and executing what we are required to do in our various roles in our personal and professional lives earns us the trust of others.

There was once a cold storage company with large walk-in freezers. The workers used to come in for the morning shift at 8 AM and leave at 5 PM. On a particular day, a manager went inside a freezer for a routine inspection, and was locked inside accidentally. He tried to open the lock but failed. He feared that he would freeze to death when he heard someone unlocking the door from outside.

It was the watchman.

Grateful, he asked the watchman what made him check the freezer. After all, it was not a part of his daily tasks. The watchman said, *"Every day you wish me when you come and wish me when you leave. This morning, I remember you had wished me while coming but I did notice you leaving. It made me come here to investigate because I feared for the worst."*

Helping others –

Whatever be our position, we can always help others either by donating money or giving our time. When someone is in trouble, we can lend a listening ear. When President Abdul Kalam was in Defence Research and Development Organisation, he had a non-matriculate driver. Kalam encouraged the driver to study for his matriculation examination and gave money for books.

He also taught the man in his spare time. With this help and guidance, the driver not only cleared his matriculation exam but continued studying and ended up with a doctorate in history and is now a college professor.

Yoga for building character

The common understanding is that Yoga is about assuming various Asanas or postures. Asanas are just one of the eight limbs of Yoga. In the *Patanjali Yoga Sutra*, the second sutra of the first section explains that the purpose of the discipline of Yoga in the words 'Yogah chittha vritti nirodhah' or '*Yoga is the control of thought waves of the mind*'.

Patanjali describes the eight limbs of Yoga as follows:

- Yama:
    - Ahimsa (not harming others)
    - Satya (being truthful)
    - Ashteya (non-stealing)
    - Brahmacharya (right use of energy)
    - Aparigraha (Non-greed).
- Niyama:
    - Shaucha (cleanliness - both physical and mental)
    - Santhosha (contentment)
    - Tapas (discipline)
    - Swadhyaya (study of scriptures)
    - Ishwara Pranidhana (surrender to a higher power).

- Asana
- Pranayama
- Pratyahara
- Dharana
- Dhyana
- Samadhi

Asana attempts to strengthen the body from inside and outside. It allows us to sit for a long time in a balanced posture so we can concentrate for long periods when we are meditating. Pranayama makes the breathing process effective. As there is a deep relationship between breath and emotion, regulation of breath helps immensely in the control of one's emotions.

The practice of the first four limbs of yoga prepares the mind to get into the fifth – 'Pratyahara', which is an attempt to insulate us from our five senses. With this one can aspire for the higher limbs leading to the deep state of meditation or Samadhi.

As good thoughts dictate good actions, control of mind leads to good thoughts and hence good character.

In Yama, 'Ahimsa' ensures that we do no harm to others. That includes using kind words, kind deeds, and having empathy towards all, and harbouring no hate for any being and the practice of forgiveness.

'Satya' builds the character of truthfulness, honesty. With practice of Satya we do not betray the trust of others, and therefore become trustworthy in the eyes of our own self and those of others as well.

Ashteya means non-stealing. Most of the crimes today are related to thefts, including cyber thefts, theft of intellectual property etc. While practicing Asteya, we do not even entertain the thought of taking something that does not rightfully belong to us.

Practicing Aparigraha, we stop coveting that which does not belong to us, and are not corrupted by any inducements.

It is possible that a youth may tend to use their abundant energy in wrong ways. Brahmacharya, the practice of sexual restraint, ensures that sexual energy is reserved for constructive purposes.

In Niyama, 'Shaucha' means cleanliness – both physical and mental. A good mind resides in a good body. This helps in imbibing positive energy, which includes helpfulness and optimism.

Santhosha or contentedness is the result. It leads to freedom from jealousy and acceptance of all.

Tapas is our ability to persist and do what needs to be done in a disciplined way till we reach our goal. Swadhyaya is an instruction to read and undertake self-study from all available sources of knowledge because books and other sources of illumination are treasure troves of transforming light. And finally, Ishwara Pranidhana - when nothing goes right despite all our efforts, why dwell on them? Leave to a higher power to solve. It will be solved. We don't have to waste our energy trying to forcibly solve it.

The third limb – Asana – helps us build a body that is good from inside and outside. Immunity, digestion and body postures improve with the practice of asansa. The body becomes capable of resisting diseases. Even the mind becomes more peaceful after practicing asana.

Asanas are therefore essential for all-round wellness.

Pranayama ensures that the body gets the necessary nourishment to energize every cell of our body. It balances the breath. It oxygenates the blood more effectively.

The result is a marked increase in vigour.

It also results in the calmness of mind as there is a deep relation between breath and mind.

Pratyahara aims at the control of our five senses – sight, smell, hearing, taste, and touch. When we are able to control them at will, there is little that can shake our poise.

The next three limbs – Dharana, Dhyana and Samadhi – help us connect with who we really are. That is a spiritual quest. When we are in a deep state of meditation, we discover our true nature, and the purpose of our birth in this world? Dwelling on this gives us our purpose in life. Once we discover our true purpose, character development becomes effortless. While all of us may not reach the elevated state called Samadhi, Dharana as well as Dhyana is adequate to anchor and transform over life.

We must encourage our children and youth to practice the eight limbs of Patanjali Yoga. The first two limbs of Yama and Niyama can be inculcated even when they are little and impressionable. This can be best done by parents. When they attain the age of 12, they can practice asana and pranayama for their own inner self-development. This helps them develop their bodies, including their muscular, cardiovascular and the endocrinal systems. Breathing becomes more effective for the one who practices pranayama. Asana and Pranayama improve their overall health. Healthy body and healthy mind go hand-in-hand. This becomes a good foundation for inculcating good character traits as the mind is now ready for the seeding of noble values.

Once the mind is ready, concepts like Dharana and Samadhi may be taught. Even if a student does not reach these elevated states, he or she is sure to imbibe the ability to control the fluctuations of the mind. This results in greater emotional awareness and control. It also helps in the formation of good thoughts and good behaviour, which, in turn, creates good character over a period of time.

Summary

A country can become strong only when the population of the country possess good character. A good society may be defined as the one where people are of good character as described at the very beginning of this chapter. Virtues like truthfulness, honesty, control of emotions contribute towards reducing crimes of passion, and inculcate a positive attitude and helping nature. The eight limbs of yoga help us to inculcate these values that form the foundation of a strong healthy society.

Wellington David Pereji

is a 61-year-old marketing and business development professional in the building materials industry from Hyderabad with a sustained passion for training. His professional experience includes 20 years in the roofing industry, 8 years in business as a turnkey contractor delivering sustainable building solutions like false ceiling, partitions, prefabricated homes, factories and roof top extensions with fibre cement boards. Now, as the Assistant Vice President of a Rs.1,100crore Company, he handles the business development and training functions of the Fibre Cement Boards division, and the team he heads is engaged in developing relationships with influencer community of Architects, Structural engineers, Government engineers, Builders and project customers in different market segments to create awareness of sustainable Fibre Cement Boards and many applications and the scope to replace conventional building materials through relevant presentations. His ordinary workday involves close interactions with his teams tasked with fulfilling his company's objectives through various training and orientation programs and joining them in making presentations to a wide range of Stakeholders. Wellington is passionate about upgrading his knowledge and he constantly employs his new learnings to add value to his teams. He is a music lover with a taste for singing and playing the harmonium. He is an active member of the local church.

10. Empower everyone to express

By Wellington David Pereji

Leadership is about empathy. It is about having the ability to relate to and connect with people for the purpose of inspiring and empowering their lives.

Oprah Winfrey (Celebrity talk show host)

To express our mind is the key thing in this fiercely competitive world. To make our presence felt when it matters most. To ideate and put forth our views. To endorse another's view or to counter it with a viewpoint that is better and more practical. To stand up for one's ideals and beliefs and face an adversary. To fight and not to be cowed down. In a nutshell, it is what we express and how we express it, that, in the final reckoning, bears testimony to our convictions, beliefs and thought processes.

Unfortunately, however, there are forces, which stunt the growth of an individual, curb his ability to grow and rob him of fearless expression. Some of these stem from one's background and upbringing while others are externally imposed upon him by various entities in society at different phases of his life. Both can be addressed with empathy, dedication and support from the community.

Team meetings, review activities and brain storming sessions are typical opportunities for expressing oneself in an office situation. Unfortunately, not everyone is in a position to make these opportunities count. It is a commonplace experience that some individuals do not partake in such conversations.

Let us call such an uncommunicative person 'Nirmal' for the purposes of this chapter. Meeting after meeting, Nirmal remains a mute spectator to the discussions at hand, only occasionally nodding or smiling to indicate his stand. On a rare occasion, he mutters a yes or a no.

The very fact that Nirmal is present at such sessions suggests that he is qualified to be there owing to his position and responsibility. The qualifications, expertise, experience and skill sets he brings to the table have earned him that position. He is excellent, friendly, supportive and adds immense value to the team. The boss is aware of this. Yet, Nirmal remains a silent spectator during the meetings.

Why is Nirmal not speaking up?

We often see individuals waxing eloquent at meetings despite their superficial and shallow knowledge of the subject. Many could even be using Nirmal as a ladder to rise in the hierarchy by passing off his ideas as their own and earning recognition as people with knowledge, ideas and solutions. We all have Nirmals in our organizations who suffer from this handicap or inability to express themselves in English either because they did not get the required education or were unable to address the shortcoming at a later date due to the pressures and demands of their jobs.

Consequently, they feel low on confidence and looked down upon. This stunts their professional growth and they also suffer from fear of judgement.

This handicap badly impedes their growth in the organization and keeps them from realizing their potential capabilities.Ironically, while flaws in communication in any other native languages are ignored, when it comes to English they are noticed and discussed. Do we allow Nirmals to fester in this predicament or address the issue and help them?

For, if they overcome their fears and gather the confidence to express their unique viewpoints, they could add great value to the team and also gain the recognition due to them. It is never too late.

There is a need to identify Nirmals in our work environments support, equip and empower them with the required tools and informal programs to help them improve their skills to write and express in English in an atmosphere of trust. This is an important responsibility of the leaders at various levels in any organization.

There are many ingenious and unique ways to address this issue. Since it is delicate, it needs to be dealt with considerable care. Professional help can be sought to deliver structured modules for the needy. An individual can adopt a colleague and help him with proven techniques to cross the threshold with consistent follow up and encouragement and make the transition smooth and successful. A personal touch makes the whole exercise enjoyable and rewarding for both.

A framework which identifies and acknowledges the need to equip employees or team members, gives the support needed to achieve a decent level of fluency to write and speak in English, which makes a huge difference to the individual and the organization. It will have positive spiral effect on the deliverables. Especially in the digital space, the need for reasonable fluency of English cannot be over emphasized.

Can we take a 'Each one Teach one' pledge and make a difference in a subtle and confidential way in some Nirmal's life and career?

This act of generosity can go a long way in empowering such Nirmals.

Let's take a look at the 'Left in The Lurch' phenomenon with the help of a case of Std. VI student in a reputed private school.

Nischal is a studious boy who has consistently figured in the top 3 in his class so far.

However, he drops his grades gradually and by the end of the year, his performance becomes lacklustre and his confidence hits rock bottom. A teacher who taught Nischal in Std V analyses his dipping performance graph and identifies that the problem lies with his English learning.

Nischal's current English teacher has a stringent method of teaching, which allows little room for imagination and personal expression. The expectations of the teacher are high on all fronts and failures are dealt with harsh treatment like shaming and shouting in front of the class. All this takes a toll on Nischal's confidence and self-esteem. Eventually, it reflects in all aspects of learning and results in low grades in all the subjects.

With no formal education, Nischal's parents were of little help in this situation. Nischal completes his schooling and joins the only college which is willing to take him in on the basis of his low grades.

Nischal's story could have been different had the management, with the help of his teacher, addressed the issue in time with empathy and facilitated a comfortable pace for Nischal to catch up with the requirements and allowed him time for adjustment and recovery.

This is a very common reason why bright students from other mediums of education do not make it to the mainstream of life, where the expectations are somewhat fixed in the area of communication skills.

We, in leadership roles in diverse fields, can play a catalytic role to empower the Nirmals and Nischals under our charge. With access to managements of the schools our children go to and other learning institutions in our spheres of influence, we can make a difference especially to those from the underprivileged sections of society. To start with, we can sensitise people in authority to the importance of this crucial issue of m1aking our wards capable of expressing themselves and contribute our mite to their empowerment.

There is also a scenario where people lack the ability to express themselves in any language for a variety of reasons.

Chary is a small-time carpenter. He runs a workshop inherited from his father. Very diligent at work, he does what is promised. A stickler for keeping his word, he delivers on time, invariably. He has developed a good base of clients with his reasonable charges. Yet he finds himself at the receiving end from both his customers and labourers. Customers pay him short, often getting more work done than what was agreed upon, causing Chary to spend extra time, materials, and wages to his workers. His labourers, on the other hand, take advantage of his gentle nature. They bunk work on and off and refuse to take pay cut for the days they are absent. Many customers do not pay their dues and continue to get fresh work done. He eventually runs into a spiral of debt and his business collapses.

This is a regular scene in our environments. The second generation gets into the business without understanding the dynamics of the trade, finance, communication process and courage to express their rightful concerns. They just operate mechanically without any mentors and resign themselves to their fate. They are very touchy about exploring other profitable business options which their current location can yield. They would rather continue with the traditional business and get wiped out by the ever-changing currents of public preferences, introduction of new products and new methods of customer service. There is scope for a Chary to stay afloat by taking up a job to support himself but the pride of being a businessman prevents him from looking at possible options, which can be profitably leveraged with his basic skills.

Is there hope for people like Chary in our communities, vicinities and environments?

Many youngsters, school/college dropouts, unemployed youth cheated by scamsters, become victims of bogus schemes. They are outsmarted by unscrupulous partners whose only idea is to grow at the expense of others. The world is full of dejected adults waiting to be helped. They have immense potential, skill sets, social skills, technical skills, empathy and team spirit within themselves. A helping hand at a crucial juncture can harness their potential and put them back on track for a new beginning.

Can we be change agents? Individually, or as a part of a community, we can bring about a transformation in the lives of such people. An effort can be made to develop a social framework to create an awareness of their ecosystem, enlighten them of their basic rights, and build the ability to voice their concerns. They can be made aware of the recourses available and emerging trends in business in areas like competition, products and services that impact their existence and position in the value chain. Thus empowered such businesses have higher chances of exploring possible ways of forging new relationships, staying relevant and protecting their client base. The community's organisational strengths, knowledge bank, diversity of experiences and scope for offering mentorship to help the needy through informal fora can well be the source of empowerment that enables them to be more articulate and seek solutions within the community.

On the social front, one's inability to express oneself and be assertive breeds a community of ubiquitous bullies. Their existence pervades all sections of the society. It starts at schools. The bullies have a special ability to target their prey.

They zero in on candidates who do not react or retaliate. They shun those who respond and possess the social skills to muster support from others. Unchecked, the bullies thrive and continue their subtle and open tactics on soft targets and inflict far reaching psychological injuries on young minds, which stunts their personalities.

Such bullying sows the seeds of the fear of judgement, low self-esteem, depression and many unhealthy coping mechanisms that can cripple a person mentally.

A voluntary effort to curb this menace in the formative years of learning in schools in our environments with proper sensitisation of teachers and management to the issue and helping them with proper tools of counselling to nip the issue in the bud can go a long way in developing well-rounded personalities for our wards.

This bullying of new students by their seniors is an organised activity that is called ragging. This practice is rampant as one rises to higher levels of education in professional colleges and universities. Till some time ago this continued with license, as it were, with successive batches taking their rightful turns to mete out the treatment to their juniors, creating sadistic vultures in the campuses. It is not difficult to recount the incidents of suicides, depression and students dropping out of courses after being scarred by this bullying, which has destroyed many promising careers and shattered the dreams of the family. Thankfully, the government has put stringent regulations in place that can take severe forms like rustication of the ragging students that has put a brake on this shameful but widespread practice.

Ragging does continue in subtle and open forms in many institutions of learning. There is a huge opportunity for change agents to make a difference in this area by creating awareness of the rights of the victims to express their anguish and avenues for redressal and counselling of perpetrators as well.

Student hostels of any form are infested with bullies. They feed on the captive inmates for extended periods of time and make life difficult for the victims. Bullies ganging up and exploiting the victims is a common menace. Another opportunity for the change agents to step in and facilitate awareness of the crime and make counselling tools and legal remedies available to all stakeholders. The administrators of the hostels in our environments also need to be provided with adequate support.

Bullying also manifests itself among siblings, between spouses, parents and children and many relationships in the society. Bullying damages the very fabric of the family and stifles the natural flow of communication and expression, which is vital for healthy living.

A bullying parent or an elder sibling at home is among the prime reasons for a stunted communication skill or an inability to express oneself for fear of being judged & ridiculed.

Then there is the spiritual bullying indulged by some spiritual leaders and religious gurus. They exploit the trust reposed in them by resorting to a style of leadership which reflects genuine care, ethics, and morals of highest standards, which in effect is a clever ploy sometimes to sustain the trust and obedience of the followers. It is a common experience across various religious institutions to find leaders resorting to manipulations, suppressions, exploitations and various other tactics to muzzle the voice and instil fear into the hearts of their flocks and cleverly push their hidden agendas. As these associations and relationships are very long, these oppressive tactics impact the ability of their followers to express themselves in a normal way and renders them mute affecting their basic personality. The followers are forced to accept the situation for fear of rejection and subtle forms of condemnation. The vulnerability is the highest in this domain as the followers permanently lower their guards and chose to be in perpetual silence. We can recall innumerable instances of Sadhus building ashrams, amassing wealth, forging nefarious political relationships & exploiting the devotees in various ways. It is time change agents rise up in this delicate domain to awaken the masses to the truth of the situation and support the masses to articulate their feelings and help them to be discerning and emancipate them from these unhealthy and vicious bondages.

Finally, we have organisational bullying, which exists as a culture or style of hierarchy across the organisations. It manifests itself in different forms like harassment, animosity, discrimination, spreading canards, public slighting, insults and insinuations, and denigration of ideas and contributions. They are actually traps into which many victims just walk into. The effect is far reaching and inhibits the productive abilities of the victims who refrain from expressing themselves due to the fear of being judged, misunderstood & alienated. This is serious limitation affecting one's ability to communicate & connect with people, add value, perform, grow, motivate and contribute to the rise of the organisations they serve.

In conclusion, it is very important that every voice in the society gets a patient hearing, an opportunity and a platform to grow as a healthy community. There is an acute need to consciously facilitate and encourage expression of individual ideas at homes, places of learning, social institutions & organisations and also identify the obstacles, forces and situations that hinder fearless expression   and through focussed and consistent efforts create inclusive and non-judgmental spaces which foster free expression of ideas and development of well rounded personalities to relate to one another effectively to build strong communities. Every reader has an opportunity to be a '**Change Agent**' in his or her own community to empower everyone to express and cause them to **RISE and SHINE.**